THE
WINGTHORN
ROSE

THE
WINGTHORN
ROSE

A Story of Transgression, Redemption and the Power of Love

Melvyn Chase

SANTA FE

Sunstone books may be purchased for educational, business, or sales promotional use. For information please write: Special Markets Department, Sunstone Press, P.O. Box 2321, Santa Fe, New Mexico 87504-2321.

Book design I Vicki Ahl
body typeface I CG Omega
Printed on acid free paper

Library of Congress Cataloging-in-Publication Data

Chase, Melvyn, 1938-
The wingthorn rose : a story of transgression, redemption, and the power of love / by Melvyn Chase.
    p. cm.
ISBN 978-0-86534-630-7 (pbk. : alk. paper)
1. Redemption--Fiction. 2. Conduct of life--Fiction. I. Title.
PS3603.H3794W56 2008
813'.6--dc22
                                          2008020116

Published in

WWW.SUNSTONEPRESS.COM
SUNSTONE PRESS / POST OFFICE BOX 2321 / SANTA FE, NM 87504-2321 /USA
(505) 988-4418 / ORDERS ONLY (800) 243-5644 / FAX (505) 988-1025

 *With love to Matthew and Rebecca, the next generation of dreamers*

Pennington

Lucas Murdoch had never heard of Pennington, Connecticut, but as he drove through the town, he began to feel at home.

On the outskirts, he passed a deserted red brick factory, the windows of its eyes nailed shut with weathered boards, its vacant parking lot still protected by a steel-mesh fence, its empty guardhouse watching Route Forty-Six, its barren loading docks waiting for phantom shipments.

A little further down the road, in boxy one- or two-story buildings: a real estate agency, an auto repair shop and a mail-order catalog fulfillment center.

A small town, too far from Boston or Hartford or New Haven to become a suburb, too poor to hold onto ambitious young people. A small town like Shelby, Pennsylvania, where Lucas had grown up.

Turning south off the road, he passed a general store that also served as the local post office. He entered a neighborhood dense with shrubbery and massive, centuries-old oak trees crowded together so tightly their branches twisted around each other in awkward, frozen intimacy.

It was mid-morning on a Wednesday, early in May.

He drove at random, eventually circling back to Route Forty-Six and going north across the highway, up a steep hill, until he reached the end of the street at the gate of a hilltop estate. He could see the broad-shouldered, three-story, white house from the road: it looked weary and in need of repair.

Pennington. Hushed, empty streets. Sullen, styleless homes and a tired, old mansion. Shabby stores. A dark-stone, somber church.

A broad street running south off the highway led him to the oak-shaded village green. A concrete-and-brass monument squatted in the grass, remembering an event that history only briefly noticed. And facing each other across the green: the Public Library and Town Hall, built in the late 1800s, dull, undignified, sagging with age.

City people lead private lives, Lucas thought. Their eyes tell you nothing. Cities keep secrets.

Suburbs share that secret life. The nourishment, the spirit, of suburban people flow from the secret heart of the city.

In towns like Pennington or Shelby, Lucas thought, every life intersects every other life. Every life history is woven into all of the others, generation after generation, a tapestry of memory. Everyone knows more about you than they would ever say. You are never a stranger.

For Lucas, Pennington was perfect. He would stop here for a while.

He drove to a brick-and-aluminum diner, Sarge's Diner, on the south side of Route Forty-Six near the center of town.

When he got out of his car, he hesitated. Without a trace of warmth, his deep-set, frosted gray eyes followed the careless drift of powdery clouds. He listened intently to the faint murmur of insects and distant traffic.

Taking several deep breaths, as if he were at the starting line

of a race, he ran his fingers through his thick, gray, close-cropped hair.

The first day. Listen. Watch.

Lucas was fifty-three years old, but his angular, handsome face was surprisingly smooth. Six feet two inches tall, slim and broad-shouldered, he walked toward the diner, his stride relaxed and athletic. By the time he reached the glass-paneled door, his eyes seemed less opaque, more accessible.

Inside, Sarge's Diner was traditional: behind a counter that ran the length of one wall, a rectangular, glassless window opened onto the kitchen. Booths lined the opposite wall. A blackboard at one end of the counter announced the day's specials. He could have predicted that.

Near the entrance, a fleshy woman in her early fifties sat behind the cash register, staring out the window in front of her. She didn't look at Lucas when he entered.

"Sit anywhere you like," she said, without expression or tone, as if the words were a formula she had memorized.

Two men were in a booth; a third at the counter. A husky, blonde waitress lounged behind the counter, leaning on her elbows, taking deep, hungry drags on a cigarette.

Lucas sat down in the booth behind the two men. Old-fashioned ceiling fans, groaning softly, circulated the pleasant, mingled aromas of coffee, bacon and onions.

The waitress inhaled a heavy dose of smoke. Then, gently, almost reverently, she rested her cigarette in an ashtray and walked over to Lucas's booth.

"G'morning," she smiled, and handed him the menu. "Coffee?"

"Yes, please."

In the next booth, the man facing Lucas was watching him intently. His thick, red hair overpowered the narrow planes of his face.

A crown of fire.

His dark eyes glowed behind thick, steel-rimmed glasses. *Fire and ice.*

The red-haired man said to his companion, "There'll be Hell to pay now," but he kept watching Lucas.

His companion said, "I'm not so sure, Henry. People like him always get away with things."

The waitress sighed, "It's a shame. For all of us," and brought Lucas a cup of coffee. "Have you decided?"

"The breakfast special. With sausages, please."

"He's a coward," Henry said, "a liar." He smiled, nodded his red head. "They'll nail him now."

The waitress went to the window behind the counter and called out Lucas's order: "Sarge, the special with sausage."

Sarge was bald, burly, red-faced.

An ex-prizefighter's face? Placid, scarred, still dangerous.

Henry looked over at the man who was sitting at the counter and said, "What about it, Joey? How do you feel about our dear President?"

Joey spun around on the stool and smiled, as if Henry had just told a joke.

"Why should he care what I think about him? Shit, I never even vote."

The waitress repeated, "It's a shame."

Joey shrugged. He was handsome and solidly built, neatly dressed in tight-fitting black slacks and a pastel shirt.

At first, Lucas thought he was in his twenties. But then he noticed the cracks in the façade: thin wrinkles across his forehead and around his eyes. The dull, dyed blackness of his slicked-back hair. The quick, furtive glimpses at himself in the mirror on the far wall.

Lucas sipped his coffee.

Henry said, "What is it, Joey? Judge not, lest ye be judged?"

Joey shrugged, glanced at Lucas as if for sympathy, and turned back to the counter.

Henry looked at Lucas again, hesitated for a moment, and then asked, "Do you have an opinion, sir?" (The "sir" sounded like an insult.)

Lucas smiled and shrugged.

He answered, matter-of-factly, "I just try to take care of my own life. That's enough to keep me busy."

"Right you are," Joey replied. "That's enough to keep anybody busy."

Henry shook his head. "Busy? That's all you do: keep busy?"

You want to embarrass me, don't you, Henry?

Lucas smiled again and looked down at his coffee.

"What a way to live!" Henry said.

Lucas nodded, looked up, shrugged again.

Henry dismissed him with a slight wave of his hand.

No mercy. No compassion.

Henry changed the subject.

"What are you and Billy going to do about the factory?" he said to his companion.

"I don't know. We're working on it. Maybe we'll come up with something at the meeting tomorrow."

The other man's voice sounded unpleasant to Lucas: harsh and flat, as if it were being forced through a strainer.

He's careful about what he says.

The waitress brought Lucas his breakfast and refilled his coffee cup.

Sarge left the kitchen through a double-door behind the counter, poured himself a cup of coffee and came into the dining area. He sat on one of the stools, facing the booths. The waitress

returned to her post behind the counter and lit a fresh cigarette from the embers of the one still in the ashtray. She drew in the smoke gratefully, as if it were fresh air.

"Clinton isn't so bad," Sarge said. "He's been a pretty good President."

Henry made no challenge.

"Could be."

Henry picks his fights carefully.

"What about Jack Kennedy, for Chrissake?" Sarge asked. "He wasn't a saint. But I liked him."

"Bad men can do good things," Henry replied. "But I'd rather see good men do them."

Sarge didn't agree or disagree.

Good and bad aren't that simple, huh, Sarge?

The other man in the booth had turned to face Sarge. He had a sullen, fine-boned, passive face that would have been more attractive on a woman.

"Ernie and I were talking about the meeting tomorrow," Henry said.

Sarge frowned, and sipped his coffee.

"You're wasting your time. She doesn't care what you think."

"Will you be there?" Ernie asked.

Sarge shook his head.

"We could use your advice," Henry said.

"I just gave you my advice. What're you going to do? Sign a petition?"

Sarge laughed and added, "Why bother?"

He finished his coffee, turned to the waitress and held out his cup for a refill.

There was a pause in the conversation. Lucas swallowed a forkful of eggs and sausage, and drank some coffee.

 12

He waited.

Then he looked at Henry, who was watching him again, and asked, "I wonder if you could help me out?"

Henry's eyes scanned Lucas's face.

Lucas didn't offer him any clues.

"You need directions?"

"No. I know where I am. This town is a lot like the one I grew up in."

"Where was that?" Sarge asked.

"Shelby, Pennsylvania."

Henry looked around suspiciously.

"Anybody ever hear of Shelby, Pennsylvania?"

"No."

"No."

Lucas smiled. "I guess it's as famous as Pennington, Connecticut."

Sarge was the only one who smiled back.

Lucas spoke slowly, deliberately pausing between the sentences: "I've traveled a lot. I was in sales, working out of New York City. My job kept me on the road most of the time. I retired a while back. Now I'm thinking about settling down."

"Why not go home?" Henry asked. "To Pennsylvania?"

"I don't like going backwards. This town will probably do just fine."

"I wouldn't count on that," Sarge said. "Towns like this don't welcome strangers with open arms. You should know that. I'm from New York, too. We've been here ten years and they still call us The New Yorkers."

Joey laughed. "Goddamn New Yorkers!"

"And I'm a special case," Sarge said. "My father grew up here."

"I don't mind being an outsider. You can start calling *me* The

New Yorker, if you want to. Anyway, it would be the same for me in Shelby. My mother and father died years ago. I have no brothers or sisters. And I never got married. I'm an outsider everywhere. So I can put down roots wherever."

Henry's eyes narrowed.

"You make up your mind awfully quick."

Lucas nodded and smiled.

The waitress came out from behind the counter. "You got to be kidding. Jesus Christ. Go someplace where there's something to do."

Sarge put a large, gentle hand on her arm. "Lucille, relax. Please."

She turned away from Lucas. "I'm sorry, Dad."

"That's all right."

Dad. He came here from New York City. Why?

"Money's not a problem," Lucas said. "I've got a pension. It's not a fortune, but it's enough to pay the freight. I might even look for a job here. But first I have to find a place to live."

"What did you have in mind?" Ernie asked. "You want to buy a house?"

Sarge aimed a warning finger at Ernie.

"You'd better be careful. Ernie's double poison: he's not only a lawyer, he's a real estate agent."

Everyone laughed, even Henry.

"I don't think I can afford a house. Anyway, it's more than I need. I'm just looking to rent. Is there a boarding house in town?"

Ernie shook his head. "No. No apartments. No condos. Except . . ."

He looked at Joey and asked, "What do you think, Joey?"

"It's fine with me. But Fay's the one you have to talk to."

"It sounds like you've got a room available."

"Maybe. My sister Fay and I have a house with a separate

14

apartment, a small one my mother lived in for a while, after she got sick. She died a couple of years ago. The place is furnished, has a stove and a refrigerator. A separate bathroom. It's not bad."

"Sounds promising. I'd like to take a look at it." He slowed the pace of the conversation by sipping his coffee for a moment. "Of course, I don't expect you to trust me, just like that. I'll give you the name of the company that handles my pension. They can tell you I'm on the level. You can get their number from the phone company, so you're sure it's not a set-up. I'll call them first and tell them to give you whatever information you need."

"I'll take care of that, Joey."

"Okay, Ernie. But first, we've got to talk to Fay."

"Why don't you take . . . What's your name, Mister?"

"Lucas Murdoch."

"Why don't you take Mr. Murdoch over to see Fay?" Ernie suggested. "While you're doing that, I'll check him out."

"Okay," Joey replied.

Henry commented to no one in particular, "He's been here for half an hour and he's ready to settle down. He's got all the answers. 'Here's the name of my banker. Give him a call. Rent me a room. And I'll unpack my bags.' He's a salesman, all right."

"I'm not rushing things," Lucas said. "I've been thinking about this for a long time—a couple of years. I guess I've been looking for Pennington, and I didn't know it. I found it today, and I want to stay."

"Henry gave me a hard time, too," Sarge said. "He gives everyone a hard time."

"Is there a phone I can use?" Lucas asked.

Sarge pointed to a door at the far end of the counter. "Yeah. There's an extension in the office in back of the kitchen. It's private. Go ahead. Dial nine to get an outside line, and one for long distance."

"What's your last name, Ernie? So I can tell them who's going to call."

"Hynes."

"Thanks."

The office was small, windowless. Several photographs hung on the wall opposite the cluttered desk. One showed Sarge in a policeman's uniform, posing with another policeman in front of a patrol car on a New York City street. There were family shots of him, his wife (the cashier in the diner) and his daughter, Lucille, all looking much younger. On the desk was a more recent photo of Lucille and a five- or six-year-old boy.

Lucas called his financial advisor, gave him detailed instructions, and returned to the dining room.

Henry stopped speaking in mid-sentence.

Joey seemed uncomfortable, but he said, "Let's go see Fay."

"Ernie, you'll want to get in touch with Archer and Fitzgerald in Manhattan," Lucas said. "They're on East Fifty-Eighth Street. Tell them you want to speak to my financial advisor."

"I'll do that right now."

Joey walked toward the door and waved his hand. "Come on, Mr. Murdoch. We're going to the library."

In the parking lot, Joey said, "We'll take my car," and pointed to a shiny, spotless, new station wagon with simulated wood panels and a Dealer's license plate.

"If you're in the market for a car, let me know. I work for the Ford dealer in Fulton—that's a few miles east of here. I'll make it worth your while."

"I'll keep that in mind."

Joey handed Lucas a business card:

Fulton Ford
For the Deal of A Lifetime!
Joey Geneen, Sales Manager

As they drove east on Route Forty-Six, Lucas was organizing what he had seen and heard. The hard work would begin later. The patterns were still only dimly outlined, but he was already energized, enjoying every new moment, every new fragment of information.

"Your sister, Fay. She owns the house?"

Joey nodded.

"Yeah. I left town when I was eighteen. Joined the navy. I was in Nam for a while. On a carrier. I was a mechanic. It was toward the end of the war, and I didn't really see much action. But it was more than enough for me. After the war, I figured I would stay in the service. It wasn't a bad life. I traveled a lot. I retired a few years ago. Fay went to UConn. She came back home right after college and became a librarian. She never got married. And when our Mom got sick—Dad died a long time ago—she moved into Mom's house, set up the apartment there on the ground floor, so Mom wouldn't have to walk up stairs. She took care of Mom for years."

And loved every minute of it?

Joey made a right turn off the road and followed a tree-lined street to the village green, parking in a lot behind the Pennington Free Library.

Lucas followed him inside.

The walls were paneled with dark wood. Bookshelves and massive tables and chairs were carved from a lighter shade of wood. A thick, deeply worn maroon carpet covered the floor.

Lucas sniffed the warm, silent, sluggish air.

Old leather bindings, old wood, old times.

They walked through the virtually empty reading room to the reference desk in the rear. A wooden name-plate was centered on the desk: F. Geneen.

 17

The woman behind the desk was thumbing through a book, making occasional notes on a yellow legal pad. Probably in her early forties, her dark hair was short and thick and streaked with gray, and she was wearing a brown shirtwaist dress that made her blend into the background.

Lucas thought, *It's as if she's saying, "I'm not really here. I'm not anywhere."*

She looked up, ready to be helpful, and saw Joey. Helpfulness melted away. Frown lines in the corners of her mouth deepened.

Joey smiled at her. No smile in return.

Her eyes drifted to Lucas. A rimless pair of glasses framed her dark brown eyes and long, thick lashes.

"Can we talk to you for a minute?" Joey asked.

"Let's go to the lounge."

She stood up. She was tall—taller than Joey—narrow-hipped and long-legged, and she moved easily and economically.

An athlete. A runner, maybe.

She turned, leading them to a door marked Employees Only. Opening it, she motioned them inside.

The librarians' lounge was a smaller version of the reading room, somber and dark. Two huge, leather-covered couches stood catty-corner on one side of the room. On the other side, three bulky leather chairs surrounded a small, round table. No one was there.

Fay sat in one of the chairs. Joey and Lucas sat opposite her.

She wears very little makeup. Her skin is clear, the color of outdoors.

"What do *we* want to talk about?" Fay asked.

She's watching Joey like a frog watching a dragonfly.

"First, Fay, this is Lucas Murdoch."

Lucas smiled and nodded, but Fay took no notice.

"Mr. Murdoch is retired. He used to live in New York City.

He's thinking of settling down here. He's looking for a place to stay."

No response.

Lucas studied her features. Her nose was a little too long, her mouth too full, her chin too strong—but the sum of the imperfect parts was attractive.

"He's got money," Joey said. "A pension. Ernie's checking that out."

She looked down at the table-top for a moment, then looked back at Joey, waiting.

"We were talking—over at Sarge's—about whether you might want to rent the apartment to Mr. Murdoch."

"What did you decide?"

Joey shook his head. "It's not up to me."

She turned to Lucas and asked, "Why do you want to live in Pennington? There isn't much going on here. But I'm sure you know that."

"I guess I'm tired of big cities. I grew up in a small town. I'd like to be back in the kind of place I remember."

He smiled, his expression a mixture of hopefulness and concern.

"I don't know if I want a stranger living in my house."

"I'm very quiet. I won't play any loud music. Or invite anyone to the apartment."

"How do I know that's true?"

"Ernie's checking on him," Joey said.

"Can he find out whether Mr. Murdoch drinks? Or plays the drums?"

"He's just checking on whether he has money."

She repeated the word "money" softly, and frowned.

She needs the money.

"I have a decent pension, and simple tastes," Lucas said.

"The apartment would be my one luxury."

"I don't know," she said, without much energy.

"We could do it on a trial basis—for a month, say."

"You would have to pay part of my electric bill in your rent, and part of the fuel bill in winter time. And you'd have to have your own phone."

"That's okay."

She looked down at the table-top. "I don't know."

"What would you consider a fair price?"

She frowned.

"It's really just two and a half rooms and they're not big: a bedroom, a combination living room-dining room, and a kitchenette. It's furnished. And I keep it clean. I'm not sure why."

Lucas nodded.

"I could take you over to see it," Joey said.

"Three hundred dollars a month. That's fair, I think."

"It sounds fair to me. And, if you change your mind, I'll leave. I don't need a lease. We can keep it on a month-to-month basis, if you like."

Joey was nodding.

"I don't know," she said. "You'd have to supply your own linens and towels. But there are dishes and pots and pans you could use."

"Why don't we give it a try?" Lucas said.

"I'd need a few days to get things in shape."

"He could stay at the motel in Fulton," Joey said.

"If you mention Joey's name, they'll probably give you the room for half price."

Joey smiled nervously.

"Show him the apartment. If Ernie says he's okay, I'll try it—for a month."

Lucas extended his hand. "Thank you."

20

Fay hesitated, then grasped his hand. She had a strong, aggressive grip. Her skin was cool and dry.

It begins.

Again, the rose garden. Thousands of rose bushes all around him, packed tightly against each other. The blood-red blossoms were thick-petaled and heavy, but all the branches stood up stiff and straight, stretching high above his head. He was running on a narrow, twisting, dirt path. He was naked and barefoot. His bare arms brushed against the bushes on each side of him. Every bush he touched pierced his flesh with its thorns and then withered and blackened and died. His blood, thin and pink and watery, streamed down his arms and dripped off his fingertips. He looked behind him as he ran. He was leaving a clear trail: withered, dead rose bushes and, on the dirt path, two muddy streams of blood. He smiled. Whatever was hunting him could track him easily, no matter how long he ran, or how far he traveled. That was a comforting thought.

As Lucas opened his eyes in the darkness, the motel room came into focus around him. He was breathing heavily, sweating. He felt the throbbing of his heartbeat deep inside his head.

Yes, it had begun.

2

The Cascades

Six-thirty a.m. Sunday morning.

It was still cool, surprisingly cool for May. Lucas had been awake for almost an hour, lying in bed on his back, watching the shadows on the white ceiling, listening to the small sounds that floated through the silence.

If he was alone, early morning was his best time. He remembered, sometimes he planned.

If he wasn't alone, early morning was when he tried to forget.

He sat up and looked around him at the apartment in Fay Geneen's house. The furniture was functional and bland. There were two dark prints on the living room/dining room walls. A faded still-life painting hung over the bed. The living room carpet was a half-hearted imitation of an Oriental rug, and even less thought had been given to the dark braided rug that covered the bedroom floor. The bathroom was equipped with the chrome bars that ease the movements of elderly people.

A generic apartment.

He wondered if the rooms had been as barren when Fay's mother had lived here. Or had Fay stripped it of its humanity when her mother died?

For Lucas, the apartment was ideal. It was temporary. It gave him nothing.

He got out of bed, smoothed out the blanket as he always did. He was naked. He went to the bathroom, showered, and brushed his hair with a few quick strokes of his fingers.

His breakfast was a glass of orange juice, a blueberry muffin and a multivitamin pill.

Lucas went into the backyard through the door that opened onto the concrete patio, furnished with a dark green wrought iron table and chairs.

He stretched his arms over his head, bent over and, keeping his knees locked, touched his toes ten times, then went around to the front of the house.

Fay Geneen was walking up the street, a few yards ahead of him. He ran to catch up to her.

She was wearing a gray sweat suit and sneakers. She walked quickly, fluidly.

At her side, he fell into the rhythm of her stride.

"Would you mind if I tag along?"

"It's more than two miles."

He acknowledged the challenge: "I'll do my best."

She glanced at him out of the corner of her eye.

"We don't have to talk, do we?" she asked.

"No."

She nodded.

They followed the street uphill, for almost ten minutes, passing a few other houses, until they came to a wider, winding street that formed a "T" in front of them. Lucas recognized the cross-street. To the left it led up to the mansion on the hill. She turned right.

23

"This is called Schuyler's Trace," she said. "It was the first street in town, before there was a town."

He didn't respond.

A cool, soft breeze stroked his face. The sky was a clear, brittle, early-morning blue.

"In the seventeen hundreds, before the Revolutionary War, Hans Schuyler cut the Trace—just a path through the woods—built a farmhouse on the hill and cleared the land around it. Then he plowed and planted his crops."

"You're talking."

She looked at him, but he continued to look straight ahead, unsmiling, keeping pace with her.

"We'll cross here and take that street to the Cascades."

"The Cascades?"

"It's a preserve that belongs to the town. There's a stream running through it and a waterfall—the Cascades—at the eastern end. We can follow a path that winds around through the woods. Lots of hills. It's a good workout."

They continued to walk uphill for a few more minutes and then came to a second "T." Beyond was a broad stretch of forest. Tucked into the western end of the woods, just across the street to the left, was "Smythe's Garden Center."

Fay led Lucas to the right of the center, onto a well-worn dirt path leading into the preserve.

Under the trees, it was almost cold. Lucas shivered.

She picked up the pace.

"If Schuyler started this town, why isn't it named after him?" he asked.

"He was Dutch, and the English weren't about to let him give the place a Dutch name. Schuyler didn't care. The Dutch are very good businessmen. And very tight with their money."

"Murdoch is a Scottish name. I understand perfectly."

She smiled.

"Pennington was an English settler with a small farm, and he took great pride in his name. Hans Schuyler is supposed to have said, 'Never mind about pride. I'd rather have property.' He got what he wanted. Eventually, Schuyler bought the whole town. Even the Pennington farm. This was always his town. Most of it still belongs to his family."

"Is that their house on the hill?"

"Yes. The Grange. But there's not much left of the Schuylers. An old woman and her granddaughter."

They walked silently through the shaded woods, into a clearing now and then, and back into the cool shadows.

At first, the sound of flowing water was distant and vague. Then it began to gain volume and clarity, until it became a steady rumble. Then, through a stand of trees, he saw a narrow, twenty-foot-high waterfall cascading over rough boulders, scattering the morning light.

The path led up a hill, across a stone bridge over a stream, down to the other side of the waterfall and back toward the entrance to the preserve.

"Have you settled in?" she asked.

"Yes. I've opened a checking account at People's Bank. I guess I'll need a new driver's license and registration, but there's no hurry. I found Appleby's and bought all the basics. I've already cooked a few meals. And I've bought an electric coffee maker. And an electric frying pan, which I use for practically everything."

A long pause.

"My drums were in storage, but they should be here by Tuesday," Lucas said.

"I can hardly wait."

"The only thing I need now is a library card."

"Stop in tomorrow and I'll take care of it," she said as they reached the edge of the preserve.

When they arrived at the house, she asked, "Would you like a cup of coffee? It's already brewed."

"Yes, thank you."

She led him through the living room into the dining room. Motioning to the table, she asked him if he wanted cream or sugar.

"Black."

She went into the kitchen.

He sat at the table and examined the dining room furniture. It was antique, but graceless. Family hand-me-downs, no doubt. An enormous breakfront dominated one wall, displaying a delicate set of china dinnerware. The chair he was sitting in was cushionless and uncomfortable. The table was a dark, clumsy slab of wood, fringed with carved chains of flowers and supported by bulbous floral columns.

Fay returned with two cups of black coffee, gave him one and sat down opposite him. She sipped hers, looking down into the cup, then glanced up at him.

"I guess Joey won't be joining us?"

She shook her head. Frown lines appeared at the corners of her mouth.

"You're not likely to see my brother on Sunday morning. Not around here, anyway."

"I hope you didn't mind me tagging along this morning."

"No."

"I've been thinking about getting a job. Any suggestions?"

She shrugged. "What can you do?"

"I've been a salesman most of my life. But I'm adaptable. And I don't need to be challenged. I wouldn't mind putting stuff on shelves or unloading trucks. I have my pension to keep me warm. I just want to make a few extra dollars. Pocket money."

She watched him over the rim of her cup.

"That's all you want?"

"That's all I want."

"I'll ask around."

He had finished his coffee.

"Would you like another cup?"

"No, thanks."

He stood up and added, "Do you walk every morning?"

She nodded.

"Would it be okay if I came along once in a while?"

She nodded.

"Just don't bring your drums."

He smiled.

On Tuesday afternoon, Lucas sat in the sun out on the patio, reading a library book. It was a warm, comfortable day.

Joey Geneen came out of the house through a sliding door that connected Fay's kitchen to the patio. Lucas watched him over the rims of his reading glasses.

Joey was wearing threadbare jeans, a wrinkled tee-shirt and sandals. His hair was combed but he hadn't shaved. A cigarette drooped between his lips.

Lucas read the cigarette's smoke signal, echoed by Joey's eyes: "Don't make too much noise. I'm hung over."

He was carrying a coffee pot and two cups, which he carefully set down on the table.

He sat down opposite Lucas and asked, "Y' want a cup?"

Lucas closed the book and put it on the table.

"Yes. Thanks," Lucas said softly. "Black is fine."

Joey laughed. "Black is mandatory."

"Day off?"

"Yeah. I worked this weekend."

Lucas sipped his coffee and waited.

Joey stared at the sky as if he was trying to remember something. He looked down at Lucas's book.

"What're you reading?"

"It's about Eisenhower and Montgomery during the Second World War."

Joey looked at the sky again.

"Military shit. You been in the service?"

"The Army." He added, casually, "Vietnam."

"Like I told you, I was in the Navy over there. But the war was almost over by then."

"You didn't miss anything."

"It must have been pretty bad."

"It could have been worse. I could have been killed."

"I was in the Gulf War, too. Just ferrying troops in."

"When did you retire?"

"Five years ago. Maybe I should have re-upped. Maybe I should have been a *thirty*-year man."

"What made you decide not to?"

"Don' know. Some things I do very carefully. Like buying a pair of slacks, or a shirt. I can look around for weeks 'til I find the right one. But if it's something important, I usually make up my mind just like that." He snapped his fingers. "My first wife—we were having breakfast and she said something that really pissed me off. So I told her I wanted a divorce." He snapped his fingers again. "Just like that."

Joey stretched and yawned. His face was pale and deeply lined, a wintry counterpoint to a Spring day.

He laughed. "My second wife did the same thing to me."

Lucas nodded.

"You ever been married?" Joey asked.

Lucas shook his head.

"You ever been close?"

"No."

"Well, twice is enough for me. Shit, that's enough for anybody."

Lucas waited.

"I don't like women," Joey said. "I love to fuck them, but I don't like anything else about them. I never did. It's like they're all working from the same plan but they never tell us what it is. Know what I mean?"

Lucas just smiled.

"Like my mother. No matter how I screwed up, my mother always thought I was hot shit. My father died when I was a kid. I hardly remember him. And Mom just let me do whatever the hell I wanted to do. She never complained. Never got mad at me. She didn't want me to join the Navy, but she never told me that. She told Fay, but she never told me."

Lucas nodded.

"Fay's another fucking mystery. She went away to college and I figured she'd stay away. Like I did. She got an education. She had no ties here. She and Mom weren't exactly buddies. But she came back. I don't know why. She's been here all these fucking years. Took care of Mom."

"Did you ever ask her why?"

"We don't talk much. She wouldn't tell me anyway."

"Did she ever ask you why you came back?"

"Yeah. I told her: it's home."

Joey poured them both another cup of coffee. He picked up the library book and looked at the cover, upside down, and returned it to the table.

"I don't read much. A mystery or a spy story once in a while."

"I like true stories."

"Y'know, you can't believe everything you read."

"You're right, Joey. That's the fun of it. When you read what's supposed to be history, some of it's true and some of it isn't." He tapped the book on the table. "Eisenhower thought he knew how to win the war. And so did Montgomery. If you read Eisenhower's book, Montgomery was wrong. If you read Montgomery's book, Ike was wrong. And there are all kinds of opinions in between."

"So how do you know who *was* right?"

"You dig. You peel away the lies. You keep digging. If you're patient enough, you can usually find the truth."

"Too much work," Joey said.

"Maybe."

"Too deep for me."

Lucas downed the last mouthful of his coffee. "It's just a game."

"Just a game," Joey repeated.

Later that afternoon, Lucas walked to the waterfall by himself.

Insect voices hummed in the air. A Babel of mismatched, dissonant birdsongs joined them.

Squirrels rushed through the branches overhead, leaping from tree to tree. Lucas could hear the hollow hoof-falls of deer, hiding in shadows.

The sounds heightened the stillness.

He watched the waterfall leap into the air and crash into the stream below, an endless watery suicide.

His gray eyes mirrored the sun-and-shade patterns of the forest around him. He felt completely alone. Completely at ease.

This would be a place to die. To disappear.

He turned and walked off the pathway, deeper into the woods. He changed direction constantly, finding open spaces between the tree-trunks, the bushes, the undergrowth. He stopped abruptly, listening. He had heard a faint new sound, the sound of bells.

He stood still, waiting for that sound again.

Only the insect voices, the dissonant birdsongs, but not the bells. After a few minutes, he began to walk again, and then he heard the bells again.

He looked up. There, like ripe silver fruit, hanging from a branch of a nearby tree, twenty feet from the ground, was a cluster of wind chimes. A squirrel running up the bole of the tree and back down again must have shaken the branch, sounding the chimes.

Wind chimes in the middle of a forest.

Who climbed that tree?

Who left behind that quiet music?

Does it mark a place to remember? A secret place?

He looked around on the ground and found a small stone. He aimed it carefully, threw it and hit them—too hard. The slim tubes crashed together, jangling harshly.

Lucas nodded and smiled, as if a question had just been answered.

On Thursday morning, Lucas went back to the waterfall. This time with Fay.

She was quiet as they approached the preserve.

There was a trace of coolness in the air as they entered the grassless, leaf-shaded areas in the woods that the sun couldn't touch.

"There's a side road—a loop that goes into the forest and then comes back again onto the main pathway—near the Cascades. Are you in the mood for a longer walk?" she asked.

"Sure."

They surprised a trio of deer grazing in a small clearing. Three tapered heads swiveled toward them, three pairs of cautious, dark brown eyes watched for a moment. Then, in graceful arcs, the three leaped away from the clearing, tawny streaks disappearing into the shadows.

After a long pause, Fay said, "You asked me about where you might look for a job. I've heard that someone's leaving the nursery—the one we pass on the way here. It's the kind of thing you said you wouldn't mind doing: fetch and carry, that kind of thing."

"Sounds good."

"It won't be available for a week or so. But Henry Smythe said you should come in and talk to him."

"Henry Smythe? Red-headed guy?"

"Yes."

"I met him at Sarge's Diner, the day I came to town."

"He's not exactly a charmer."

"He sounded like a preacher."

"He almost became one. He holds Bible study classes—unofficial ones—at his house."

"How does your minister feel about that?"

"I don't have a minister. But I know that Reverend Stokes doesn't like the competition."

"I'm not a churchgoer, either."

She didn't respond to his confession.

"Henry doesn't pay much attention to the nursery. Six or seven years ago, he hired a manager: a black man named Leo Sage. From Chicago. Smart guy. Leo runs the whole operation."

"I haven't seen any blacks in town."

"Leo's the only one. There's a black neighborhood in Fulton, but Leo doesn't hang out there, as far as I know. Doesn't drink. Doesn't gamble. He's a loner. Very quiet. Keeps to himself. I guess in a town like this, that's not surprising."

They followed the loop deeper into the forest, then made a wide turn and started back toward the main pathway. A few paces on, he could hear the rumble of the Cascades.

"The trees have the right idea," Fay said. "They don't get old."

He didn't respond. He let her words float in the air.

She's so accustomed to walking here by herself. She may have forgotten that I'm here.

"They live a lifetime every year. Dying every winter. But there's always another spring. Another chance to be young. Hundreds of chances."

She turned and looked at him.

He wasn't ready to agree or disagree. Not yet.

He smiled at her: a neutral, passive smile.

Now she was sorry she had shared her thoughts with him. Her dark brown eyes reminded him of the deers' eyes: alert, always anticipating flight.

She turned away.

They walked back in silence.

The next day, Lucas went to talk to Henry Smythe. When he entered the main building, a stocky black man was behind the counter speaking on the telephone, adding up a nearby customer's bill, using sign language to tell a young man in coveralls how to line up flowerpots in a display, and smiling a greeting to Lucas.

The first three tasks completed, the man looked at Lucas and asked, "Can I help you?"

"From what I've heard, you must be Leo Sage."

The man nodded and smiled slyly. "Now, how in the world did you know that?"

Lucas returned the same kind of smile. "Fay Geneen said you were in charge of everything at the nursery."

Leo laughed. "What can I do for you?"

"My name is Lucas Murdoch. I'm here to see Henry Smythe about a job."

"Yeah. Henry told me you'd be in. He's not here right now, and I'm not sure when he'll be back. But hiring and firing is my responsibility."

"It figures."

"Why don't we go to the office and talk." He called to the young man who was eyeing the display of flowerpots with pride, "Tom! Take over the counter. I'll be back in a little while."

Lucas followed Leo down a corridor to an airy, high-ceilinged room. Sunlight poured through three huge windows that looked out on several greenhouses, racks of well-watered flowering plants in clusters of purple, yellow, white and pink, and rows of saplings thrusting out of burlap-wrapped globes of earth.

Leo sat down behind a large, oak work table and motioned for Lucas to sit across from him.

"Coffee?" he asked.

"No, thanks."

Leo looked out the window for a moment. Lucas studied his face. It was a strong face, broad-boned and confident. His hair was sprinkled with gray. But his eyes didn't tell you anything.

"I'm not sure you'll really be interested in this job."

"Why not?"

"It doesn't pay much. It's part-time, afternoons and half a day on Saturday. And it's really just grunt work."

"Sounds like the ideal job for me."

Leo watched him for a moment.

He's looking for signals. He's used to looking for signals. And he's used to hiding his own.

"I'm retired. I've got a pension. This isn't a second career. Just a way to make a few extra dollars."

"Henry told me about you. He says that you're living at Fay's place."

"She's the one who told me about the job."

"You plan to stay in Pennington for a while?"

"Maybe for good."

"Really?"

He's not comfortable with me.

"Why not? I grew up in a small town. And you're living here, aren't you? Fay said you're from Chicago. If you can be happy here, why can't I?"

"How do you know I'm happy?"

He's probing.

"I don't. But I think *I* can be."

Leo looked out the window again, then back at Lucas.

"You'd be doing the kind of things Tom does—that kid you saw setting up the flowerpots: stocking shelves, watering plants, loading customers' cars, cleaning up, and whatever else I can think of. I'll give you five dollars an hour. You work every weekday afternoon from one o'clock to five. Every other Saturday morning, from eight to noon. And it won't start for another week—a week from next Monday."

"Sounds fine. By the way, I don't know anything about flowers."

"Don't worry, you won't be giving anyone gardening tips. You can leave that to me. And we'll try to educate you as we go along."

Leo stood up and extended his hand.

A friendly gesture, but he still isn't comfortable with me. Good.

Lucas shook his hand.

"I'll see you in a week," Leo said. "The first day you come in, you can fill out your tax forms and any other paperwork."

"Thanks. I'm looking forward to it."

"See you then."

3

Memory Lane

That evening Joey knocked on Lucas's door and asked him for a favor.

"What do you need?"

"I made this date for tomorrow night. With a girl I met at a place I hang out in. In Fulton."

Joey was leaning against the door frame. He seemed uneasy.

"You can come in if you like."

"That's okay. Anyway, this girl said she would meet me on Saturday night—if I got a date for her friend. I guess she thinks she's safer on a double."

He added, with obvious pride, "I got a reputation."

Lucas smiled.

"My friend Stan said he would go. He works with me. But he told me today he couldn't make it. And I've got to show up with a date for her friend or I'm up shit's creek."

"You want me to go with you?"

"Yeah."

"I'm a little old for that sort of thing."

"It's not a big deal. All you've got to do is talk to the other girl. Dance with her a few times, if you feel like it. You and I won't be leaving together: I'm sure of that."

"I guess you deserve your reputation, huh?"

Joey basked in the thought: "I guess I do."

"How old are these girls?"

"Well, they're not teenagers. Shit, no. Early thirties. How about it?"

Lucas said, "Yes," but he wasn't sure why.

I suppose I can learn more about Joey. But there isn't really much to know about him. Do I just want a night out?

"Thanks," Joey said. "I appreciate it."

He turned away, then back. "You better take your own car, right?"

"Right."

On Saturday night, following Joey's shiny Ford, Lucas drove east on Route Forty-Six to the next town, Fulton, which was bigger, newer, and flashier than Pennington. In the crowded town center, branches of major chain stores invited shoppers to come in. Past the shopping district, on the eastern edge, restaurants and bars flanked the highway. They stopped at a dimly lit place called Memory Lane.

Lucas parked his car next to Joey's.

Live music swirled into the parking lot. Amplified guitars twanged a monotonous rock melody while a bass guitar pounded out a throbbing, bone-deep rhythm.

"Thanks, again," Joey said.

Memory Lane was divided into three sections. To the left, a

long bar ran along the wall. In the middle, there were ten or twelve tables. To the right was a huge dance floor, with the bandstand—a raised platform—against the far wall.

The bar, the tables and the dance floor were crowded. Joey pointed to one of the tables, where two women were sitting. One of them, a plump blonde in a red dress, was watching the door. She waved at Joey. He smiled and waved back.

The women stood up as they approached the table.

Joey put his arm around the blonde and kissed her on the cheek.

"Jill, this is my friend, Lucas Murdoch."

Jill smiled at Lucas. "Nice to meet you."

The other woman introduced herself to Lucas, "I'm Margot Sinclair."

Her voice was so soft the music almost obliterated it.

Jill added, "That's Margot with a 't' at the end. French Canadian."

Margot extended her hand.

Lucas shook it.

"Hi. I promise not to pronounce the 't'."

Margot smiled and whispered a polite "Thanks."

They sat down. Joey moved his chair closer to Jill and put his arm around her waist. She didn't seem to mind.

Margot was a slender, petite brunette with a face he would have turned to look at even if she were a stranger he saw at a restaurant or a cocktail party.

She has a beautiful mouth, beautiful eyes.

From her already weary expression, Lucas sensed she was there for the same reason that he was.

He leaned toward her so he could be heard, and asked, "Do you live in Fulton?"

"Yes. Not far from here."

"Margot and I work together," Jill said.

He could hear her voice easily over the music.

"What do you do?"

"We're executive assistants at a law firm in town."

Executive assistants. We used to call them secretaries.

Joey grabbed a waitress going by and ordered beer for the table.

"I haven't finished the one I got," Jill said.

Joey kissed her again. He whispered something to her. She laughed.

Lucas asked Margot, "When did you come here from Canada?"

She shook her head.

"I'm American born. My father was French Canadian."

"Sinclair is English, isn't it?"

"His real name was St. Claire. But he anglicized it."

"Anglicize." Nice word.

The beer arrived.

Joey kept nuzzling Jill as he drank his beer. Kept whispering to her.

"How long have you known Joey?" Margot asked.

"About a week."

She seemed surprised.

Lucas explained, "I'm a substitute for the original double date. It was supposed to be a younger man."

She looked at the dance floor, at the band, at Lucas, but not at Joey and Jill.

"I haven't had much practice at this for a long time," Lucas said.

"Neither have I."

She raised her glass in a toast to him, but the gesture was

40

more resigned than friendly, as if she were saying, "We'd both rather be somewhere else."

He returned the gesture.

"See you later," Joey said, and led Jill onto the dance floor.

"Are you a car salesman, too?"

"No. I'm renting a room at Joey's house. That's how he knows me."

"What do you do?"

"Actually, I'm retired."

"What did you do?"

"I worked for a big company. Did what I was told. Made a living. Left with a pension. An early retirement package."

"And settled down in Pennington, Connecticut?"

"Why not? I was born and raised in a small town."

"You don't look small-town to me."

"I guess this is what they mean by a second childhood."

"You still haven't told me what kind of work you did."

"I was a salesman, but I didn't sell cars. I traveled a lot."

"A traveling salesman? Sounds like the set-up for a dirty joke."

"Right."

"You don't like talking about yourself, do you?"

"I'm not a very interesting subject."

She smiled and asked, "What did you sell?"

"Computer software. For business information systems. Accounts payable, inventory, et cetera."

"How old are you?"

"Fifty-three."

"How long have you been retired?"

"A few years."

"What's a few? Three? Five? Twenty?"

"More than three, less than twenty."

That's not exactly what I told people in Pennington. That was careless.

"Retired so young? You must have a hell of a pension."

"Enough to pay for an apartment in Pennington. This isn't Hilton Head."

Margot shook her head.

"You sound like someone who's been practicing his answers," she said.

For a moment, Lucas was off-balance.

"I'm not sure I understand you," he said.

She sipped her beer, gesturing toward the dance floor, where Joey was pressed tightly to Jill.

"I didn't want to go out tonight. Knowing Jill, I could imagine the kind of guy I'd end up with. Someone like him."

She paused, then said, "You're not like him. So far."

She stretched and hunched her shoulders.

"I'm tired of dating," she said. "I never thought sex was all that great and I'm tired of the song and dance leading up to it."

She emptied the beer glass and poured a refill.

"I was married when I was twenty. I was s-o-o-o in love. After a few years, I got tired of him. He was too predictable. I decided to go back to school and get my degree. He didn't want me to. I was already too smart for him. He was an accountant who couldn't pass the CPA exam. I got my degree. And he left me for a much dumber woman. Prettier, but dumber."

"You have no children?"

"I can't have children."

"I'm sorry."

"Don't be. I'm not the mother type. I may not be the wife type, either."

"When did you get your divorce?"

"I didn't. Catholics don't get divorces. Besides, I'm enjoying the fact that he's living in sin."

"That's not very Christian of you."

"Granted."

"If you didn't want to go out tonight, why are you here?"

"Jill wouldn't leave me alone. I work a few feet from her every day. It wasn't worth arguing about."

Joey and Jill returned to the table briefly, drank some beer, whispered to each other and returned to the dance floor.

"I'm not sorry I met you tonight," Margot said. "So far. It's too noisy in here. My ears hurt. Do you want to go for a walk, or something?"

"We came in separate cars. Joey insisted."

She laughed.

"We can drive someplace, if you like," Lucas said. "Someplace quiet. Or I can take you home."

She thought about it for a minute.

"There's a coffee house a few minutes from here. It's not very fancy, but there's no music. In fact, there are fake tapestries on the wall that absorb sound."

"Let's go."

"After that, you can take me home."

They waved to Joey and Jill on the way out. Joey smiled conspiratorially. Jill just smiled.

The coffee house was a tired relic of the Sixties. The pony-tailed proprietor and his wife were gray-haired Flower Children whose petals had faded long ago. But the place was quiet and they could talk without shouting, while they drank their espressos.

Lucas tried to relax, but he felt uneasy.

"You're a college graduate. And you're working as an executive assistant. Are you looking for something better?"

"Not at the moment," she replied.

"What did you major in?"

"Economics."

He grunted. "Difficult and boring. You're a better man than I."

Margot nodded, as if she agreed with him. Her eyes were dark blue and opaque, like the tinted windows of a limousine: a guarantee of privacy.

"Now back to questions," she said. "So you retired early, but you said you didn't make a fortune?"

"I don't need much to get along."

"That's another packaged answer."

Lucas tried to read her expression.

Aggressive, but not unpleasant. She's playing with me. I should reciprocate.

"Lucas, would it be all right if I called you Luke?"

"I've been called worse."

"Luke, I guess you'd rather not tell me much about yourself. But I'd like to see you again, anyway, even if you get to know all about me and you still remain a man of mystery." She paused a moment and looked at him earnestly. "Since my marriage broke up, I've met a lot of men. I'm not the answer to anyone's prayer. I'm not beautiful or sexy. Like I said, I'm not even that interested in sex. But most of the guys I've gone out with aren't good enough for me. I suppose all the good ones go to Boston or New York."

"Could be."

"I used to be bitter about my marriage, but what's the point of that? It doesn't do you any good. So I let it go. I stopped thinking about it. I started enjoying things: a glass of wine, a good meal, a

movie, a book, sleeping late on Sunday morning. Pleasures that are easy to come by."

"What about family?"

"My folks live in Hartford now and I call them every week. I see them once in a while. My brother moved out to the west coast a few years ago, met someone out there and got married. They have a little girl. I go out to visit them every year, in the winter."

"Friends?"

"I have one very close friend. I've known her since high school. She moved to Boston, but we see each other every couple of weeks. We've gone on vacation together a few times. Once in a while, I have dinner with Jill and a couple of the other women at the office."

"And, now and then, you go out on a terrible date."

"Ain't that the truth."

"And you don't consider this one of those terrible dates."

"I don't. Do you?"

He knew that he should back away from her. She didn't fit into his plans.

Be careful.

"No, I don't either."

"You know," she said, in a reassuring voice, "I'm not looking for anything permanent, if there is such a thing. So I'm not dangerous."

"So far."

She smiled and echoed, "So far."

She opened her handbag and took out a small note pad and a ballpoint pen. She wrote her name, address and phone number on a sheet of paper, tore it off the pad and handed it to him.

"For your Rolodex."

Later, he drove her to her home on a quiet street about a mile north of Route Forty-Six. It was a small, old-fashioned New England saltbox. A wrought iron bench, painted white, stood on the lawn a few feet from the front steps.

At her door, she shook hands with him and said, "I had a nice time tonight."

"For a change?"

She laughed. "For a change."

"So did I."

"Call me."

Her voice was very soft and her hand was small and fragile.

"I will."

When he was driving back to Pennington, he shook his head a couple of times, as if he were disagreeing with someone.

I shouldn't call her. No reason to call her.

He thought of the wind chimes, hanging from a branch in the forest.

Music where no one can hear it. What a waste.

He remembered the harsh jangling when he hit the chimes with a stone.

He decided to call her anyway.

Although he walked through the Cascades at the usual time on Sunday, Monday and Tuesday morning, he didn't meet Fay again.

I've known her for only a few days and she's already trying to avoid me. That's encouraging.

On Wednesday morning, it was warm and summery, so he wore shorts and a tee-shirt. Halfway to the waterfall, he started to

46

run. His stride was smooth and practiced.

He drew the heavy, tree-scented air into his lungs, and felt the gentle fingers of a self-created breeze. He moved through variegated patterns of sun and shadow, from light to darkness and back again.

He remembered the fierce joy of running beyond his endurance, beyond thought, beyond feeling, running until there was nothing but running—no earth, no sky, no sun, just the painful rhythm of step after step after step.

What was chasing him then?

And now?

4

Let's Get Lost

On Wednesday afternoon, he went to the library.

A poster on a bulletin board near the entrance announced a screening of Eisenstein's film, *Alexander Nevsky*, at a community college a few towns away. He had seen the film when he was an undergraduate. He couldn't remember anything about it.

Fay saw him approaching her desk and tried to look friendly.

"Good morning. Do you have a minute?" Lucas asked.

"Sure."

"Thanks for your help. I got that job at the nursery. I start next Monday."

"For some reason, Henry seemed very interested in hiring you."

Lucas smiled.

"He's looking forward to sticking it to me."

"Why? He doesn't even know you."

"We met once, remember? He thinks I don't care enough about good and evil."

"But he hired you anyway."

"Actually, Leo Sage did. Henry wasn't there."

"I guess you're Henry's latest project."

"He wants to save my soul?"

"No doubt about it."

"Maybe I'll go to one of his Bible classes."

Fay just shook her head.

"I haven't seen you on your morning walk lately," Lucas said.

"I guess I've been a little lazy."

"I miss the company. Will I see you tomorrow?"

"Probably."

She looked around the library, as if she was hoping for an interruption, but all she saw was the clerk on duty, and an elderly woman reading the *Hartford Courant* at a corner table.

"Joey told me about Saturday night," she said. "I can't believe you let him fix you up."

"His friend had cancelled and he needed a replacement. I just went along for the ride."

She responded too quickly. "Joey said you and your date skipped out on him," and then she tried to look unconcerned.

"The place was too noisy. So we left. Went to a coffee house for a while."

"It doesn't sound like a total disaster."

"It wasn't."

She began to ask another question, but stopped herself.

Lucas waited for a moment.

Then he asked, "Are you busy a week from Sunday?"

She reacted slowly, as if she couldn't make the transition to a new subject.

"Sunday?"

"Yes. A week from this coming Sunday."

"Why?"

"They're showing *Alexander Nevsky* at Exeter Community College. At two in the afternoon. Would you like to go?"

"Well . . ."

"I can pick up the tickets. We could have dinner afterward."

"I don't know."

"Why not?"

"All right. Yes."

"Good."

"The last time I saw that movie, I was in college."

"Me, too."

He smiled at her, said, "I'll see you tomorrow," and walked to the shelves.

After a few minutes, he found what he was looking for: *The New Bible Companion: a Guide to Understanding the Scriptures.*

An hour later, Lucas was sitting at the table on the patio, reading and drinking beer straight from the bottle. His eyes scanned the pages of the book he'd checked out, picking a paragraph here, a phrase there.

After a few minutes, he realized he couldn't concentrate. He put the open book face down on the table, shut his eyes and pressed the cold bottle against his forehead.

Then, reaching for his cell phone, he pushed a quick-dial button and raised the phone to his ear.

After two rings, a woman's voice said, "Spector's. Can I help you?"

"This is Murdoch."

"Just a minute, please, Mr. Murdoch."

Music on hold for a few seconds, then: "Hello, Mr. Murdoch."

"Bernie. How's she doing?"

"Very well. She just got a promotion and a raise. And now they're mentioning her name on the program, as the news writer."

"What else?"

"She's still going out with the same guy."

"Vincent."

"Vincent. They usually end up at her apartment, and he stays late. But he never sleeps over. And she never stays at his place over night, either."

Lucas didn't comment.

Bernie said, with obvious reluctance, "And she goes to Grassmere every Friday. Never misses."

"Is the Grassmere story the same?"

"Nothing has changed."

"Anything else I should know about?"

"No, sir."

Lucas pushed the End button.

He lowered the phone and rested his hand on the table, cradling the receiver in his fingers.

Grassmere every Friday. Never misses.

He put the phone back into his pocket. He picked up the book and began to skim again, then stopped at a passage from Genesis:

"Then the Lord rained upon Sodom and upon Gomorrah brimstone and fire from the Lord out of heaven;

"And he overthrew those cities, and all the plain, and all the inhabitants of the cities, and that which grew upon the ground.

"But his wife looked back from behind him, and she became a pillar of salt."

Fay walked with Lucas on Thursday morning, silently at first. She took the longer route through the Cascades and kept increasing the pace, as if she was trying to tire him out.

He matched her silence and her pace.

When they were circling back, he said, "Yesterday morning, I ran most of the way. Did you ever do that?"

"No."

"You're in good shape. You should try it. Running really clears your head."

"My head is clear enough."

She turned to look at him and he smiled at her. "We can build up to it, a little at a time."

She nodded once, acknowledging that he had just reversed their roles: now *he* was challenging *her*.

"I assume you've run the Boston Marathon several times," she said.

"I never even tried."

"Why not?"

"Because I can't win."

"That's not the answer I expected."

He ignored her comment and asked, "How about it? We don't have to run full out: just trot. From here to the big oak tree" (he pointed) "up on that hill."

"All right. Let's go."

She began tentatively, at a slow trot, staying alongside him. She started to pick up speed running downhill and he followed suit. He could hear the quickened rhythm of her breath. They hit the lowest point at the base of the first hill and started up the slope of the second. Her breath became more labored, but she didn't slow down. She was straining to move ahead of him, but couldn't.

She groaned softly, but kept running.

They reached the oak tree and kept running.

Now they were on the downhill side. She was gasping for breath but kept running.

There was a long straightaway at the base of the hill.

He stayed at her side.

She began to slow down and then stopped, suddenly, leaving the path and dropping down on the dewy grass.

Her face was flushed as he joined her. She was breathing hard. And he thought that this was the first time he had seen her at ease.

She hunched forward, hooking her elbows over her knees.

She said, without resentment, "You're not even out of breath."

"Give it a couple of weeks and you'll be running circles around me."

She groaned: "Sure."

He stroked the damp blades of grass with his fingertips, letting the warm silence of the woods embrace him. He closed his eyes and listened for the wind chimes, but the air was still and all he could hear was bird and insect noise.

He almost forgot that Fay was there. Almost forgot he was there, as well.

"I enjoyed that. Thanks," she said.

He opened his eyes. She was watching him intently. And, for the moment, she was too comfortable to hide her interest.

"You're welcome."

"Tomorrow, maybe we'll do this again."

"You're on."

She stood up.

"When we get back, I'm making scrambled eggs and sausage," she said. "After I take a shower, of course. Would you like that?"

"You bet."

On the way back, he could feel a new intimacy and a new tension between them.

They had breakfast in the dining room, her hair still damp from the shower. She was wearing a pastel-flowered summer dress and sandals. Her dark eyes seemed a little softer behind the austere, rimless glasses. She was still reserved, but in a different way. He waited for her to take the lead.

"Do you really want to work at the nursery? You can do better than that."

"It'll be fine. It's only a few hours a day."

"Wouldn't you rather do something more interesting? I'm sure you could find a better job around here: in Fulton, maybe. Or at Exeter College."

"It'll be fine."

"What will you do the rest of the day? What *do* you do the rest of the day?"

He answered her only with a smile.

"I'm sorry, it's none of my business."

"That's all right. When my drums arrive, you won't have to ask again."

"Ah, those fabled drums!"

He laughed, paused a moment and said, "I spent most of my life working very hard. Long hours. Weekends. I'm trying to depressurize. I read. Drive around. Find a little lake somewhere and watch the water. As you know, I stop in at the library, now and then. I go to Sarge's Diner for lunch or dinner and I eavesdrop. Ernie Hynes is usually there with—what's his name? Billy Miles?"

"He owns the liquor store. And he's been the First Selectman for as long as I can remember. Nobody else wants the job."

"They're always talking about the old factory."

"They're trying to persuade Emily Grant—Emily *Schuyler* Grant, who lives at the Grange—to sell the property to a client of

theirs. A developer who wants to build a shopping mall. Emily's not interested. She doesn't need the money. She'd rather leave things the way they are."

"And I'd rather have a job I can do on automatic pilot."

She shrugged. "As you say, it'll be fine."

He nodded.

"Now that we've settled my future, what about yours?"

"I'm doing work that I enjoy. Living in my home town, in the house I grew up in. I'm healthy. And I don't have to see that much of Joey."

She smiled and added, "I'm even in training to become a long-distance runner. What more could I ask for?"

"That's a good question. But I can't answer it."

She looked at her watch. "There's no doubt about my immediate future: it's almost time to open the library. I'd better get going."

"See you tomorrow morning," he said. "Ready to run."

She groaned, "I can hardly wait!"

That evening, after dinner alone, Lucas sat in the stiff armchair in the living room of his apartment, drinking coffee and staring at one of the dark prints on the wall behind the sofa. It was a sepia-toned portrait of a slender young woman walking through a gloomy, deep-shadowed forest. She was looking back over her shoulder fearfully, as if she saw something following her, beyond the frame of the image. Or was it only fear itself that she saw?

The cellular phone was on an end table beside the chair. Lucas looked at it for a moment. Then back at the picture on the wall, expectantly, as if he thought that the frozen drama would continue—that the young girl's pursuer would have moved forward into view.

He picked up the phone and pressed a quick-dial button.

"Hello."

"Margot?"

"Yes."

"It's Lucas Murdoch. How are you?"

"Fine, Luke. How are you doing?"

"Fine."

"I'm glad you called. And surprised."

"I said I'd call you."

"I know. But I thought you were just being polite."

"Being polite is not one of my virtues."

"Are there any other virtues I should cross off the list?"

"I'll leave that up to you."

"Okay. By the way, how's your good friend, Joey?"

"As charming as ever."

"I can believe that."

They both laughed.

She said, "I'm not busy Saturday night."

"No blind date?"

"Not yet. How about you?"

"I think I've got a date. Do I?"

"Yes."

"Anything special you'd like to do?" he asked.

"We could fly to Paris and stay at the Ritz."

"My passport just expired."

"In that case, how'd you like to go to a jazz club? Do you like jazz?"

"I did. Years ago."

"There's a place just outside of Fulton called Babe's. Nothing fancy, like you'd find in New York City. It's owned by a lady in her seventies—Babe, of course—who says she sang with Chick Webb's band long, long ago. Maybe she did. Anyway, she thinks she did.

56

She gives young musicians a chance to play there. She doesn't pay them much, but they have an audience. Sometimes you can see some real talent."

"What about dinner?"

"Do you like Italian food?"

"Yes."

"I know a nice place in town. I'll take you there."

"I'll pick you up at seven."

"I'm looking forward to it."

He started to answer, but didn't.

She said, more softly, "I'll see you on Saturday."

"On Saturday."

He looked back at the print on the wall. Nothing had changed.

Saturday night was warm and dry.

When he drove up to Margot Sinclair's house, she was sitting outside on the white wrought iron bench near the front steps. She was wearing a simple beige dress, a string of pearls and small pearl earrings.

She stood up to greet him. Her two-inch heels lifted her closer to his eye level, but she was still so small and slender that, at first, she looked like a child pretending to be a woman. As she came closer to him, she held out her hand and watched him approach, that illusion dissolving into the early-summer air.

"It's a beautiful night, isn't it?"

"I guess so," he replied.

She laughed. "I can't even pin you down on that?"

"It is definitely a beautiful night. No question about it."

"The restaurant isn't far from here, so we have plenty of time. Would you like a glass of wine before we go?"

"Sure."

"I've got a Pinot Grigio and a Merlot. At the moment, that's my entire wine cellar. What's your pleasure?"

"Merlot."

She made a quick trip into the house and returned with the wine and two glasses on a round wooden tray. She gestured for him to sit at one end of the bench. She sat at the other end, placing the tray down between them, and poured the wine.

"To the future," she toasted, touching his glass with hers.

He sampled the wine. "This is pretty good for a two-wine cellar."

"Anything exciting happening in your life?"

"Not really. What about your life?"

She sipped her wine, savored it.

"I've been thinking about making a change," she said.

"What kind of change? What are you smiling about?"

"You looked very suspicious when I said that. The change has nothing to do with you. Not directly, anyway. On Saturday night, you asked me why I was working as an executive assistant when I had a degree in Economics. The answer is: I just wanted to drift for a while. To do something that wouldn't demand much of me."

"And now you're tired of drifting?"

"Yes. I'm afraid of what I might become."

He wondered if *he* was what she was afraid of becoming.

"What kind of job are you looking for? Secretary of the Treasury?"

"I doubt Clinton needs another woman to worry about right now."

Lucas laughed. "It wouldn't hurt to ask him."

"When I graduated from college, I worked at the headquarters of a regional bank for a while—as an economist. The job didn't pay much, but I had a chance to do what I enjoy most: play with numbers.

Modeling, forecasting, regression analysis. Music to my ears."

"I never paid much attention to forecasts. I could never get the experts to agree."

"Be careful. You almost told me something about yourself."

"We were talking about you."

"You remind me of a guy I dated last year. He was in the N.S.A. I don't know what his job was, but practically nobody knows what they do, right? Every time I asked him a question, he would stop and think for a few seconds before he answered. It was like talking to someone on one of those old satellite phones: there was always a delay between my questions and his answers. Finally, after two dates, I asked him what the hell was going on. Of course, he didn't answer me right away. He stopped, thought for a minute and told me that, when you do the kind of work he does—top secret stuff—you're always editing what you say to other people, even the people you work with. If they don't have a need to know, you don't tell them. So that's what this poor guy was doing all the time. Making sure that he didn't tell me something that was Top Secret."

Lucas smiled.

"You do the same thing to me all the time. You're not a master spy, are you?"

"If I was, I wouldn't tell you, would I?"

"I give up."

"Don't," he said quickly, and just as quickly regretted saying it.

She put her hand on his arm. "Giving up is not one of my virtues."

She watched his eyes, waiting for another signal.

He said, as casually as he could, "Why not just take me as I am? Right now, tonight."

"I wish I could. You're a very attractive man and I don't want to chase you away. But I can't help it: I want to know you better. I've spent the last few days thinking about you. Hoping you would call. Hoping you were thinking about me. But I doubted it. You always seem to have something else on your mind."

"I've thought about you, too."

He felt awkward, uncertain, as if he were an actor at the first, tentative run-through of a new play.

He put his wine glass down on the tray, leaned forward and took her hand.

"I didn't plan on meeting you," he said.

"You're kind of a surprise to me, too. But who cares about plans?"

She smiled and added, "When I was a kid, I didn't plan to be this short, but I can live with it."

"So we'll go slow. Okay?"

"Okay."

He leaned back, slipping his hand from hers.

They sipped their wine thoughtfully for a few minutes.

Then she put her empty glass next to his, lifted the tray and said, "I'll be back in a minute. We'll go to dinner."

He watched her go back into the house, smiled at her when she came out.

At the Italian restaurant, the Chianti was hearty, and the veal and pasta delicious.

The place was jammed with tables set too close together, with extra chairs added to accommodate an overflow crowd, primarily Italian families, each with several children, as well as assorted grandparents, uncles and cousins. A continuous wave of laughter, shouting and recorded music washed over them. The noise was overpowering.

After a few minutes of trying to communicate, Lucas said, loudly, "I'm glad you picked such an intimate spot."

"Sorry. I usually come here for lunch. It's a lot quieter in the afternoon. A business crowd."

He shrugged, she smiled, as they enjoyed their dinner silently.

Lucas welcomed the break in the conversation. Things were moving too quickly for him.

He shouldn't have called her. She was a distraction. And he wasn't careful enough about what he said.

But why should it make any difference? He enjoyed being with her. And it had been a long time since he enjoyed being with anyone.

As long as he didn't lose his focus.

As long as he was careful.

As long as he remembered that Pennington was the only thing that mattered.

And that Pennington wasn't the end of it.

He began to feel more at ease.

Then Margot leaned across the table, put her hand on his and asked, "Are you angry at me for bringing you here?"

He shook his head, smiled, and looked down at her hand. And all he could think about was how much he wanted to kiss it.

When they arrived at Babe's Place, it was only nine-thirty. Recorded jazz was playing over the sound system.

Babe herself greeted them at the door. She was a tall, black woman in her seventies, with deep-set gray eyes and a friendly smile.

The small club was almost empty. She led them to a table near the bandstand.

"I've got a real treat for you tonight," she said. "A young man named Marvin Connor. Blows tenor sax. Keep your eye on him. He's gonna be big someday. Soon. And he's startin' out right here at Babe's. Not in New York City, or New Orleans or Chicago, but right here. You remember that."

"We'll remember," Margot said.

Babe smiled and left.

They ordered beer.

"Do you come here often?"

"Not really."

"Why not?"

"I've been here with friends a few times. I've even come alone and sat at the bar. But I'd rather listen to jazz with someone who isn't just a friend."

"Yeah. It's very personal music."

"Too personal for us?"

In the background, a sweet, muted trumpet and a husky trombone were singing to each other. The yellow half-light splashed gold streaks in Margot's dark blue eyes and drew soft shadows on her face.

"No, it's not too personal for us," he said after a few moments.

"I just heard the N.S.A. pause. Am I being too aggressive?"

He looked away. "No."

The rest of the tables, and the bar, were filling up quickly. It was primarily a young crowd, but there was a sprinkling of older couples, too.

A few minutes before ten, Lucas heard a jazz recording he recognized: Chet Baker, long ago, singing and playing an old love song.

Lucas remembered the sound of Baker's voice—a dry, androgynous wisp of smoky melody. And his brief trumpet riffs that

compressed emotion into tight little packages.

"Let's get lost,/ lost in each other's charms./ Let's get lost./ Let them send out alarms . . ."

Lucas remembered listening to that song years ago, at the beginning of things, with someone else, stroking her hair, kissing her mouth.

"Let's get lost/ in a romantic mist./ Let's get crossed/ off everybody's list . . ."

He looked at Margot.

He shouldn't see her again.

She smiled at him. The gold splashes glowed in her eyes.

"Let's get lost."

The song was over. The recorded jazz was over. It was ten o'clock.

Babe was up on the bandstand, testing the microphone, "One, two, three. Good evening, friends."

There was polite applause.

"Welcome, everybody, young and old, to Babe's Place."

She introduced the Marvin Connor Trio.

Applause. Cheers.

The musicians were in their twenties, intense, arrogant and shy.

Lucas tried to lose himself in their sound, but he couldn't: they played hard-edged, dissonant jazz that was too far from the funky music he used to enjoy. And they improvised on original melodies, rather than the show tunes and standards he knew.

He had nothing to hold onto. He let go, drifting in the wake of the trio, trying not to think about Fay, or Henry Smythe, or Bernie Spector, or Grassmere, or the girl in the sepia print and her pursuer.

Or Margot.

He tried to imagine what she would think of him if he told her everything.

"Let's get lost . . ."

The voice of the tenor sax sliced through his thoughts. The harsh music held no welcome.

But Margot's eyes did.

They didn't say much, as he drove back to her home.

At the door, she asked, "Would you like to sit out here for a few minutes?"

Glowing softly in moonlight, the white bench looked unreal, like a fading memory.

"I don't think so."

"Would you like to come in? I could make some coffee."

"No. Thank you."

"Will I see you again, or have you lost patience with me?"

"I'll call you during the week."

She reached up and touched his face with her fingertips.

He leaned down and kissed her forehead, her cheek and her lips. Then his arm was around her waist, pulling her closer to him. Her mouth opened slightly and he touched the moist surface of her lower lip with the tip of his tongue.

She sighed, putting her arms around his neck, extending the kiss.

He pulled away.

"I'll call you."

5

The Garden Center

On Monday, a few minutes before one p.m., Lucas reported for work.

In a far corner, one lone customer was examining decorative flower pots on a display table. Leo Sage was behind the counter, in the middle of a telephone call. He nodded "hello."

Henry Smythe was there, too.

He greeted Lucas: "Good afternoon, Mr. Murdoch. I've been waiting for you. Welcome aboard."

Henry smiled. His eyes, shielded by thick, steel-rimmed lenses, remained distant and predatory. The bright sunlight seemed to set fire to his thick, red hair.

He extended his hand and Lucas shook it. Henry's grip was aggressive, almost angry, as if he were trying to strangle Lucas's fingers.

"Leo tells me that you won't mind doing some of the dirty work around here."

"That's right."

"Good. Do you want a pair of coveralls?"

"No, thanks."

Henry walked around the end of the counter. "This would be a good time to mop up the place. It's the slowest time of the day. I'll show you where the utility closet is."

He started toward the rear of the building.

"When I spoke to Leo, he said I'd be filling out tax forms today."

Henry spun around.

"No need for that. I've decided to pay you off the books."

"Really? Isn't that—immoral?"

Henry's eyes narrowed. He studied Lucas's face, searching for mockery, but found none.

"God didn't create the Internal Revenue Service."

"But shouldn't we render unto Caesar what is Caesar's?"

"Let me worry about Caesar. You worry about cleaning the floor."

He opened the door of the utility closet.

"Sweep the whole place first. Empty the dust pan into this garbage can. Then fill a bucket with hot water—the sink is over there—add some liquid soap. You'll find it on that shelf. Wring out the mop five times—five times only—and then change the water. I don't want you recycling dirty water."

He handed Lucas a broom and a wide dust pan with a four-foot-long, wooden handle.

"When you finish with that, I've got plenty more for you to do. Any questions?"

"No."

"You can take a fifteen minute break at three o'clock. There's a coffee machine in that alcove. And I bring in donuts every morning. There may be some left."

He walked away.

Lucas began to sweep, starting in one corner at the back of

the building, moving slowly, methodically, rhythmically, avoiding contact with racks and tables, collecting the sweepings in the dust pan and emptying it into the garbage can at intervals.

He thought of Fay, how she had looked this morning after their run, how she had watched him, how she had smiled at him. She was opening the gates. She wanted him to know he was becoming an important part of her life.

She was already in his orbit.

Henry Smythe? Lucas had just begun to throw him off balance. There was much more to do.

Leo Sage: he was too careful, too guarded. Lucas wasn't sure he would succeed with Leo.

And there was Sarge Schreiner, and Billy Miles, and Ernie Hynes. And maybe others, too.

It would take time. He had the time.

He thought of Margot.

He thought of the bench near her front door, moonlight-pale and hazy. He thought of her sitting there, with splashes of white in her dark eyes and soft shadows on her face.

He thought of himself sitting beside her on the bench, holding her hand, never coming back to Pennington, disappearing one morning like the moon.

"Let's get lost . . ."

He tried to erase the image.

I'll disappear one morning, but not before it's time for me to disappear.

Lucas swept and mopped, and then moved more than two dozen flower pots and urns from wooden palettes behind the nursery onto display racks and tables inside.

Henry watched Lucas closely, inspected the floor after it was cleaned, and made several suggestions about the arrangement of the flower pots and urns. At five minutes to three, Henry told him to take a break.

Lucas filled a styrofoam cup with black coffee and took a slightly stale chocolate donut from an almost empty box labeled Appleby's General Store.

He joined Henry and Leo, who were standing at the counter, drinking coffee.

"I guess you've really settled down in Pennington, huh?" Henry said.

"I guess."

"You've got a place to live, a job. A girlfriend."

Lucas reacted slowly, as if he were puzzled.

"Girlfriend? Who would that be?"

"Your landlady, of course."

Lucas smiled wryly.

"She's not my girlfriend."

"The two of you are always walking together in the woods back there. Just about every morning. Isn't that right, Leo?"

Leo nodded.

"Walking, yes. That's all we do, Henry."

"Fay must be kind of lonely. She doesn't date much. She was engaged once, a long time ago, but nothing came of it."

"She's not my girlfriend."

Henry leaned toward him and whispered, confidentially, "You're both grownups. You're both single. And you're kind of living together, right? Nothing to be ashamed of, is there? You're only human."

Henry's eyes contradicted the generosity of his words.

"We're not living together. She's my landlady. My friend, too. Nothing else."

"If those walls could talk . . ."

"They'd have nothing to say."

Henry nodded, as if he agreed with Lucas.

"Have we tired you out, yet?" Leo asked.

"A little."

"Well, you clean up better than the kids do. A lot better than Billy does."

"Who is Billy?"

"Billy, Jr.," Henry said. "Billy Miles's son."

Lucas looked around.

"Is he here today?"

"Not yet," Leo said. "He's late, as usual. He should have been here an hour ago."

"Dock him," Henry said.

"He doesn't care. We should fire him."

"No sense in doing that. His father's trying to straighten him out."

"I've heard the same story for almost two years now. And he's still a lazy kid with a smart-ass mouth."

"Don't worry about it."

Lucas wondered why Henry was so forgiving. It wasn't like him.

"I don't even bother talking to him any more," Leo said. "He's all yours."

"What's next on my schedule, Henry?" Lucas asked.

"There's a big wooden shed behind this building. We haven't cleaned it for months. It's a mess and I'm going to need the space soon for storage. There's lots of broken pottery in there, empty sacks, God knows what else. Get a pair of gloves from the utility room and clean it up. It may take you a couple of days. Put the trash in a wheelbarrow and empty it in the ditch out past the greenhouses, at the edge of the woods."

The shed was dark: a weak patch of light streamed through the one tiny, dirt-encrusted window in the wall opposite the door. Heavy dust hung in the air, laced with the acrid smell of fertilizers and chemicals and decaying flowers. Debris was scattered in piles ranging in height from a few inches to four or five feet.

Lucas began to load trash onto the wheelbarrow he had left just inside the door. As he picked through the piles, tiny, dark insect forms skittered and crawled away, fleeing into the deeper shadows.

Don't get too comfortable back there. There's no place to hide. I'll find you tomorrow, or the next day.

When the wheelbarrow was full, he pushed it through the door. The bright light blinded him for a moment.

Fifty feet or more beyond the furthest greenhouse, tall oak trees and white-barked birches hovered over the far side of the six-foot-deep ditch, which was about twenty feet wide and just as long. Nearby, mounds of dark earth surrounded an old, battered John Deere tractor with a shovel attachment—the shovel that had scooped out the ditch and would eventually bury the debris.

Like the sins of the past.

Lucas emptied the wheelbarrow into the ditch.

After work, Lucas showered and changed into clean clothes. Then he drove to Sarge's Diner. The diner was crowded.

He smiled at Ellie, Sarge's wife, but she didn't return the smile.

Ernie Hynes and Billy Miles were sitting at their usual table, deep in conversation. Ernie smiled sourly at Lucas.

Billy was a soft, fleshy man. His eyes kept scanning the faces around him, as if he expected someone to betray him. Ernie spoke

very softly, too softly to hear. But Billy's high-pitched voice pierced the background noise, although Lucas couldn't make out what he was saying.

Lucas sat at the counter. He waved at Sarge, who was working in the kitchen. Sarge waved back.

Lucas ordered a tuna salad sandwich from Lucille, and a cup of coffee.

He had almost finished the sandwich, when he felt a heavy hand on his shoulder. He looked up. Henry was standing behind him.

"Mr. Murdoch."

"Henry."

"How'd you like to join us? Ernie and Billy and me?"

"I'm just about done."

Henry's fingers dug into Lucas's shoulder.

"When you're through eating, bring over your coffee."

"Okay."

Lucas ate the rest of his sandwich slowly, washing it down with coffee. He paid his check, left a tip for Lucille and asked her to refill his cup. Then he walked over to the table where Henry sat alongside Billy, facing Ernie.

"Billy, this is Lucas Murdoch. You've seen him around town," Henry said.

Lucas shook Billy's hand, which was damp and tentative.

He sat down next to Ernie.

"You're from New York, is that right?" Billy asked.

Lucas nodded.

"Henry tells me you were a salesman."

Lucas nodded again.

"What'd you sell?"

"Software."

"There's good money in that," Ernie said.

"I did all right."

"Henry says you retired. You're a little young to retire, aren't you? You must have money."

"Enough for the way I live."

"You plan to stay here?"

"Yes, I think so."

"Mr. Murdoch grew up in a small town in Pennsylvania. Says he feels right at home in Pennington," Henry said.

He added, "And now he's got a great job at the garden center, isn't that right, Mr. Murdoch?"

"Right."

Billy watched Lucas for a minute, but he didn't ask him any more questions.

Henry leaned toward Billy and asked, "So, what's your approach now?"

"What can I do? Emily won't discuss it with me any more. And her lawyer doesn't return my calls."

"Or mine," Ernie hissed. "I passed the bar exam just like he did. No goddamn professional courtesy."

"Time is a'wasting," Henry said.

Billy nodded. "Diebold has already withdrawn its bid. Hamilton gave me till the end of June. A little more than a month."

Billy pursed his lips and rubbed his bald head delicately with the tips of his fingers, as if he was hoping to encourage hair to grow there again.

"Next door, in Fulton, they're making money," he said. "Chain stores, restaurants, night clubs. Half the people who live here work there. This town is dying."

He looked around him, angrily, as if everyone at the diner were a traitor.

Ernie said, in a hoarse, sibilant whisper, "We could turn things around, Lucas, if we could get our hands on the factory. It's

on a hundred acres, right on Route Forty-Six, perfect for a shopping mall, fast food restaurants, maybe a bowling alley."

"Billy and Ernie are on the Board of Selectmen," Henry explained. "A while back, they put out the project for bids and they found a couple of developers who have the money to buy the property and make it happen."

Billy shook his head. "But it won't happen."

"Who owns the factory?" Lucas asked.

Billy answered, "Emily Grant."

Ernie expanded on Billy's answer. "Emily *Schuyler* Grant."

"And she'd rather not sell it to anybody," Henry said.

"Why not?" Lucas asked, matter-of-factly.

Billy's voice shimmered with resentment. "She doesn't need a reason."

Ernie hissed, "She doesn't need the money."

"Years ago," Henry added, "she closed the factory and moved the whole operation down to Puerto Rico."

Billy shook his head. "She can make a lot more money down there, where they pay people three dollars a day."

Henry summed up: "In a month or so, the project goes down the drain. And we won't have another chance until Emily dies."

"And she doesn't plan to die," Ernie said. "She looks younger every year."

Henry sighed. "We've still got till the end of June."

"That's all we've got," Billy said.

Ernie got up from the table. "It's dinner time. I'm going home."

Billy did the same. "Me, too."

They walked toward the door.

Lucas stood up and started to follow them.

"Don't go, yet," Henry said. "My burger is on the way. Keep me company. Let me buy you a slice of Sarge's apple pie. Best in the county."

Lucas sat down, and ordered the pie and another cup of coffee.

Henry bit into his hamburger and chewed it with feral energy.

The apple pie and coffee arrived, and Lucas sampled a forkful.

"You're right. It's very good."

Henry nodded and bit off another chunk of hamburger.

Then he said, "Now you know a little about local politics. A shopping mall would be a real shot in the arm for the town. Of course, Billy and Ernie and I stand to make some money, too. Kind of a finder's fee."

Lucas nodded.

"You were a businessman. Any ideas about what we can do?"

Lucas decided to pretend that Henry was seriously asking for advice.

Lucas sipped his coffee, thought for a moment. "You're trying to sell this idea to Emily Grant. And she doesn't need money."

"She's got enough to last her for a thousand years. And she keeps making more, even here in town. She owns a big piece of my store. And Billy's liquor store. And Ernie's real estate agency. We all had to buy from her—or borrow money from her—or both. For our homes, too. That section south of here—the Glade—those were originally houses that the factory workers rented from the Schuylers. The people who live in them—like Leo—are still renting. She won't sell those houses. See, even with the factory closed, this is still a company town."

Lucas nodded. "It's a hard sell."

"Any ideas? About what we can do?"

The first step out of the shadows.

"Selling isn't about the product," Lucas said. "It's about the

74

customer: what she needs, what she wants."

Henry just nodded and kept eating.

"You have to find the weak spot. The place where she's vulnerable."

"What if there is no weak spot."

"There usually is."

"Okay, suppose you find it."

"You may be able to get her to make the deal."

Lucas could see that Henry was beginning to reevaluate him.

Lucas took another bite of pie and sipped his coffee.

"You don't know Emily," Henry said.

He thought it over and added, "I could introduce you. I do a lot of work for her. Take care of the whole estate, all the gardening. And I help her in the greenhouse, too. She's always trying to breed new varieties. She asks me for advice all the time. I'm over there a lot. I could take you with me, Lucas."

That's the first time he didn't call me "Mr. Murdoch."

Lucas said, "No guarantees, you understand?"

"Sure, sure. Do you think you can figure her out?"

"I don't know."

"We've got nothing to lose. What about it, Lucas?"

"Okay."

Henry squinted at Lucas, as if to get a clearer image of him.

He said, "I can tell you this. We're not sharing the finder's fee. Still interested in doing this?"

"Yes. Maybe someone else can clean the shed or mop the floor once in a while."

Henry laughed briefly, but his eyes were cold and brittle.

"Wednesday afternoon, I've got a delivery to the Grange. You'll go with me."

Lucas could see Henry wasn't very optimistic.

Tuesday night, he called Margot.

"Hi, Luke. How are you?"

"Fine. How are you doing?"

"Well, I started putting together my resumé. And I looked through the want ads in the Sunday paper."

"See anything promising?"

"There were a few possibilities."

"Banks?"

"And brokers. The stock market is so hot now, everybody's hiring."

"I suppose you could do forecasting for any kind of company."

"That's true."

"You just have to be sure the future looks rosy. Otherwise, you'll get fired."

She laughed.

He said, "CEOs decide what companies should earn. And then the accountants make it work out that way, right?"

"Has that been your experience?"

"I'm just guessing."

"Of course."

"I got a job."

"Would you hang up if I asked you about it?"

"I might."

"Tell me about your job."

"Click."

She laughed again.

"I'm just a hired hand at the local garden center."

"You're into gardening?"

 76

"I can't tell a tree from a telephone pole. But all they need is someone to clean up and carry things around and load trucks."

"It sounds challenging."

"It keeps me busy."

"Not too busy, I hope. How would you like to come over to my place for dinner one night this week?"

"You mean you don't want to see me on Saturday night?"

"I mean I want to see you every night."

He tried to find a way to answer her, but couldn't.

"I'm not a great cook," she said, "but I make a very good coq au vin."

"What night is best for you?"

"Thursday?"

"Fine."

"Do you remember how to get here?"

"I remember everything."

"I know you work in a nursery now, but please don't bring me any flowers. I'm allergic."

"I'll bring you a bottle of wine."

"Good. Seven o'clock?"

"I may be a little late. I get off work at six and I have to shower and change."

"I'm a patient woman. I'll wait for you."

6

The Grange

When Lucas arrived at the nursery on Wednesday afternoon, the truck had already been loaded for the delivery to the Grange.

"I haven't told Billy or Ernie what we're trying to do," Henry said. "The more I think about it, the less sense it makes."

"It's worth a try."

Lucas was enjoying Henry's discomfort.

It took only a few minutes to drive to the Grange. The gates were open.

Henry followed a broad driveway up the hill, around the massive white house to a parking area alongside a separate, four-car garage. There was another outbuilding, a greenhouse, in a treeless clearing not far from the house. Narrow-slatted, rolled blinds hung on the outside of the slanted glass roof.

Up close, the Grange looked threadbare, but still stark and dignified: three broad stories of traditional New England white clapboard, with forest green shutters and trim, and a dark roof with a wrought-iron, rooster-crowned weathervane perched on its highest

peak. Two sets of French doors in the rear of the house opened onto a wide veranda, with steps leading down to the grounds from both ends. The grounds extended as far as the edge of the woods, a quarter mile away. Formal, hedged gardens flanked the main house, and there were pathways and flower beds and stands of trees and fountains carefully arranged in patterns of color surrounding the house.

"Emily wants to see me at about four, four-thirty," Henry said. "We've got a lot of digging to do before then."

"We?"

Henry laughed. "If I just supervise, we'll be working until midnight. A few days ago, I cleared some spots in the beds by the house and put down lime. We'll start there."

As they were unloading flats of seedlings, Lucas asked, "Why did you use lime? Is that a fertilizer?"

"You really don't know anything, do you? There's too much acid in the soil here. The lime cuts down the acidity."

Lucas put heavy sacks of fertilizer and peat moss into the wheelbarrow and rolled it over to the border of one of the flower beds. Henry attached a long-necked sprayer head to a hose that he screwed onto an outlet in the back of the house.

They put on thick gardener's gloves. Henry showed Lucas how deep and wide and far apart to dig the holes, how to line them with fertilizer and peat moss, place the seedlings in them, and soak them with water.

Methodically, Henry catalogued the flowers—Sweet William, begonia, Shasta daisy—but Lucas didn't try to remember their names. He didn't think he'd be doing this kind of work much longer.

It was a very warm, breezeless afternoon so both took off their shirts. Henry's chest was narrow and well-muscled. The thick, red hair that covered it was soon matted with sweat.

When they had finished planting the flowers, Henry told Lucas to unload the shrubs. The roots of each were encased in a ball of soil wrapped in burlap.

"We're going to fill in the hedge along the pathway with these camellias," Henry said. "Some of them died over the winter and I've dug them out already. In fact, the holes for the new shrubs are almost ready. Put the plants in very gently so you don't damage the roots."

There were only half a dozen camellias to plant. Henry was watering the new arrivals when Emily Grant came onto the veranda through one of the French doors.

Lucas watched her approach.

She was a small, fine-boned woman dressed in tan slacks, a white, short-sleeved blouse and sandals. Her gray hair was pulled back in a tight bun. Lucas knew that Emily was in her seventies, but her face was smooth, her skin unwrinkled.

"Good morning, Henry. How are you?" she said.

Her voice was surprisingly deep and vibrant.

An actress's voice?

She inspected Lucas from head to foot, her eyes appraising his bare chest and shoulders.

"Mrs. Grant, this is Lucas Murdoch. He just moved to town. He's working at the nursery."

"Where are you from, Mr. Murdoch?"

"New York City."

"Did you own a nursery there, or work in one?"

"No. I really don't know much about gardening. I was in the software business. I was a salesman."

She raised one eyebrow. "A New York City software salesman finds happiness in a small-town garden center. That sounds like a soap opera plot."

She smiled and added, "And not a very believable one."

"It's the truth. But if you prefer, I'll make up a better story."

"I'd like that."

"Okay. I'm actually a shady financier on the run—a fugitive from the I.R.S. I'm hiding in Pennington until the Feds give up the chase."

"Is that the truth, too?"

"If you want it to be."

Emily laughed. "I prefer it."

Lucas bowed from the waist.

"Then that's what I'll be for you."

He glanced over at Henry, who was trying to make sense of what he was hearing.

Emily's smile tightened. "You know, Mr. Murdoch, around here, I'm someone to be respected. Even feared."

"Thanks for the warning."

She turned to Henry and said, "Let's go to my greenhouse. Please join us, Mr. Murdoch. You may learn something. About horticulture."

As they followed her, they put on their shirts.

Inside the glass walls of the greenhouse, the air was thick with the heavy, mingled scent of young, sprouting plants. Two roof ventilators were open forty feet away, at the far end of the building, and the roof blinds on one side were rolled down to block direct sunlight. An exhaust fan hummed a monotonous tune as it drew out the warm air. A wide aisle down the middle of the greenhouse was lined with shelves full of potted plants, beds of soil with green shoots of new growth pushing through, and racks of tiny seedlings in containers.

Emily led them to a flat, dirt-covered table, on which several small, potted roses stood, side by side. Some of them were less than a foot tall, with miniature scarlet blossoms, each with a white spot in the center. The other roses were about eighteen inches tall, with bright, reddish-orange flowers.

"It's time to take the next step, isn't it, Henry?" she asked, confidently. "You know how careful I was to keep their feet warm all winter."

Henry examined the plants carefully.

"Yes, it's time," he agreed.

Turning to Lucas, Emily said, "Roses aren't temperamental. In fact, they're pretty tough. But sometimes you have to coddle them. That's what I've been doing, to get them ready to breed. And you've got to keep their roots warm when it gets cold outside."

"It makes them more romantic, I guess."

"Actually, breeding roses is a rather cold affair. You pick one variety to be the female. You strip off the petals from each of its flowers and pull off the male organs, so it can't fertilize itself."

"So far, I don't like it."

She smiled.

"Then you wait for the female organ to get sticky."

At this point, Henry was redder than a rose.

"The suspense is killing me," Lucas said.

"And then you brush the pollen—the sperm, so to speak—from the other variety of rose onto the female organ. And *voila!*"

"A new breed."

She smiled. "I wish it were that simple. You fail more often than you succeed."

"How sad."

"Not really. Flowers don't demand emotional involvement. That's what makes them such a pleasure to deal with. When they don't come out the way you want them to, when they breed monsters, or when they die, you discard them. No funerals. No mourning. You just try again."

Henry, still a little embarrassed, said, "Mrs. Grant has been very successful in breeding new varieties. 'Emily's Prize.' 'Schuyler's Trace.'"

Emily ignored Henry.

"I don't know much about roses," Lucas said.

"Surely, you've sent them to the women in your life."

"But, to me, 'a rose is a rose is a rose'."

She turned her head to one side, like a hungry bird watching a worm come into view.

She said, "Henry, thanks for giving me the go-ahead. Do you mind if I keep Mr. Murdoch for a little while?"

"I'm not sure I . . ."

"You can get back without him, can't you?"

"Yes, of course."

"I'll see that he gets home, safe and sound."

"All right."

"See you tomorrow, Lucas," Henry said and left the greenhouse.

Emily waited a beat before she said, "You must be thirsty. I know I am. Would you join me for a drink?"

"Yes, thanks. But I really should wash up first."

"No problem. Come with me."

He followed her to the house, up the steps of the veranda, through the French doors and into a high-ceilinged, wood-paneled game room. A pool table occupied one corner, two dart boards hung on a side wall, and an elaborately-carved wooden chess set stood, waiting, on an oak table. Heavily-laden bookshelves lined the long back wall. A wide bow window looked out onto the veranda and the gardens beyond.

Emily gestured at a door. "There's a bathroom. You'll find soap and towels. What would you like to drink? I'm partial to Manhattans."

"I like mine extra dry."

"Me, too."

The sink and toilet and fixtures in the bathroom were very old, and Lucas could see that some of the tiles on the floor had been replaced: they were several shades lighter than the others. When he looked at himself in the antique mirror, his image was slightly blurry, as if he were seeing himself in the past.

He stripped off his shirt and washed his face and upper body. The soap was waxy and pink, with a raised flower on its surface. It smelled too sweet.

He dried himself with a thick bath towel that hung on an ornate rod.

He put on his shirt, ran his fingers through his hair and took a deep breath.

He wasn't tired, but he was weary. There were so many pieces to move, so many lives.

When he came out, Emily called to him from a small table near the bow window. He sat down opposite her. A tray on the table held a full cocktail shaker, two empty glasses, and a miniature bowl filled with maraschino cherries and equipped with a tiny pair of silver tongs.

"May I do the honors?" Lucas asked.

Emily nodded.

He put a cherry into each glass and poured the Manhattan mixture over it.

He raised his glass.

"To your health."

They clicked glasses and sipped their drinks.

"Just right," he said.

"How long have you been in Pennington?"

"A few weeks."

"What do you think of our town?"

"It's what I expected."

"And what did you expect?"

"A quiet place where I could feel at home."

"Where are you living?"

"I'm renting an apartment at Fay Geneen's house."

"And you're working as a gardener, even though you know nothing about gardening."

"That's right."

Emily looked out at the sky for a moment, then looked at her drink and finally looked at Lucas.

"You're not at home here. You don't belong here," she said.

"I grew up in a town just like this one."

"Maybe so, but that was long ago."

She leaned across the table and looked into his eyes.

"I can always spot a successful man. You're a successful man. What are you doing in Pennington? What's your game?"

"I don't have a game."

She laughed.

"Even a fool like Henry has a game. You certainly do."

"You misjudge me. I'm a retired salesman who simply wants to settle down in a small town like the one he grew up in."

"And I am the Queen of Romania."

"You're certainly the Queen of Pennington."

She nodded.

"You've been listening to my 'subjects'?"

"Yes. As you said, you're respected—and feared."

"And hated, too, I hope."

"You hold all the cards. You own the town. Why should they like you?"

She laughed.

"Then why the hell do they stay here? Pennington isn't a

prison. They can leave any time they want to. But they're afraid to go. The ones that stay here deserve what they get."

Lucas had finished his Manhattan. So had Emily. He felt cooler and more relaxed. He refilled his glass and hers.

Out of the shadows.

"I've been told that you're in your seventies," he said. "But you look much younger."

She sat up a little straighter. "It isn't surgery. Or a special diet. But it does take a kind of talent."

"Witchcraft?"

She smiled.

"No."

She sipped her drink and thought for a moment.

"It's love that makes people old. Love almost always ends in disappointment. If you invest yourself in someone—a friend, a husband, a child—it never turns out to be a good investment. People don't understand that. They don't learn. They waste themselves on one kind of love or another, over and over again. That's what makes them grow old."

"You've never loved anyone?"

"Only myself."

"What about being loved?"

"I don't miss it."

She smiled at him and asked, "How old are you, Mr. Murdoch?"

"Fifty-three."

"You look rather young, too."

She laughed.

"Yes, I guess I do."

He waited a moment, then said, "I'm told that the factory on the edge of town belongs to you."

"It does. At one time, most of the people in Pennington

worked there. We make women's clothing. Several different product lines. They're all doing well."

"Why did you close the factory?"

She held her glass up to the light and looked into it, as if she were reading a familiar story.

"We paid our people well. We provided free medical and dental benefits. We built houses for them they could rent for pennies—well below market price. We gave them the Cascades: it was our property and we turned it into a park. It was our money that built the library and furnished it and bought the books in it. We funded the company pension plan. And we never had any lay-offs, even during the Depression."

She paused and put her glass down on the table.

"But they weren't satisfied with the things we gave them. They tried to unionize the factory. They got more from us than they could get from any union contract. But that didn't matter to them. They wanted me to sign away my right to manage my company. That's when I moved the whole operation down to Puerto Rico. And I left the factory here as a reminder, so they could see it every day—useless and empty. They tried to take something away from me, so I took everything away from them."

"Would you like another drink?"

She nodded.

"They never give up, either. They're still trying to take something away from me—Billy Miles and Henry and Ernie Hynes. They're trying to get me to sell the factory to someone who wants to build a shopping mall."

She looked at Lucas and said, "Billy's father was our chauffeur. Henry's was our gardener. Ernie's father worked on our assembly line. I don't bargain with the servants' children."

"I think they're beginning to realize that."

Emily pointed her finger at him.

"You ask a lot of questions, Mr. Murdoch, and you're a good listener. But you haven't told me anything about yourself. Anything I believe."

"It's getting late, Mrs. Grant. It's been a long day."

He stood up.

"Do you need a ride home?"

"No, thank you. It's a short walk."

"And you're in very good shape, aren't you?"

Her smile was surprisingly seductive.

She walked with him to the front door.

As he left, she said, "Why don't you come here for dinner next week? Say, Tuesday evening at seven-thirty. Maybe I can find out more about you."

"I'm an open book, Mrs. Grant."

"But the pages are blank."

"Good night."

"Good night, Mr. Murdoch."

That evening, Lucas went to Sarge's for dinner. He knew Henry would be there, with Billy and Ernie.

Henry waved him over to their table.

Lucas sat down next to Ernie, and ordered a steak sandwich and a light beer.

Henry's eyes burned at him through the thick lenses of his eyeglasses, like the sun through a prism. Billy smiled nervously and caressed his bald scalp with his fingertips. Ernie seemed more sullen than usual.

Henry leaned forward toward Lucas and said, softly, "I never heard anyone get away with talking to Emily the way you did."

Lucas shrugged.

"What is she going to do to me? I have nothing at stake."

"What happened after I left?"

"She invited me into the house for a drink. We talked."

"I've known her all my life," Billy said, "and she never asked me to have a drink with her."

"I'm a stranger. A new toy."

"What did you talk about?" Ernie asked.

"Mostly small talk. Trivial stuff."

Henry frowned. "Drinks. Small talk."

Lucas's light beer arrived. He took a long swallow, savoring the taste.

"Is that all that happened?" Henry asked.

"No. We talked about the factory. And the shopping mall."

Lucas took another drink.

Billy tapped his fingertips on his scalp, a silent drumbeat.

"She knows what you're trying to do: take something away from her," Lucas said. "But you don't hold any cards. She's the dealer. She owns the deck."

"So we're screwed," Ernie said.

"Damn," Billy said.

Henry waved his hand at his friends. "Wait, wait. There's more, isn't there, Lucas?"

"Yes."

He enjoyed playing with their tension, feeding it, teasing it.

"This is my take on Emily."

They waited, impatiently, while he searched for the right words.

"The only way you might—might—get her to sell the factory is if she profits by it."

"But she's going to make a fortune selling the property," Billy said.

Ernie shook his head. "It makes me sick—all the money

she'll get for it. And we're getting practically nothing."

"Emily wouldn't mind making more money," Lucas said, "but she doesn't need it. You have to give her more than that."

"Did she tell you what else she wants?" Henry asked.

"No."

Lucas's steak sandwich arrived. He pulled off the top slice of rye bread, reached for a plastic ketchup bottle on the table, squeezed a thick, red wad onto the steak, replaced the ketchup bottle and reassembled the sandwich. He took a hearty bite and chewed.

"Jee-zuss!" Ernie whispered impatiently.

"First of all," Lucas said, "she should get a piece of the action. The developer can build the mall, but she has to keep a percentage of it."

He drank some beer.

"Second, her name should be up in lights—not Grant; Schuyler. The Schuyler Shopping Center, or the Schuyler Mall. Or whatever she wants. She can pick it. This town wasn't named after her family. Maybe that didn't matter two hundred years ago. I'm sure it matters to her now. You might even put up a plaque honoring old Hans Schuyler and his family."

Billy shook his head.

Lucas ate another mouthful.

"Third, one of the anchor stores should be hers, selling her stuff."

Billy almost shrieked, "No!"

"Billy, relax," Henry said.

"For Chrissake, why don't we put up a big statue of her, too?"

He kept shaking his head.

Lucas said, "She's going to win either way, Billy. But at least you can make some money on the deal. And the more people come to town, the more business there'll be for your liquor store, for

Ernie's real estate business. For everyone."

Billy leaned back, as if he had been pushed away from the table.

"Her name. Her store," he said.

"Her town," Lucas added.

"You think she'll sell?" Ernie asked. "If we make that kind of offer?"

"Maybe."

Billy shook his head. "I'll never offer her a deal like that."

"Billy, I think he's right," Ernie said. "You've always done the talking for us. You've got to do it."

"I can't. I won't keep giving that bitch more and more."

"I understand," Lucas said.

Henry pointed a finger at Billy. "I don't. What the hell does it matter to me if she makes more money—as long as I get something, too. And Lucas is right: if the mall opens, it'll mean more business for everybody. Billy, you've got to make her the offer."

Billy's high-pitched voice sounded out of tune. "I won't. Why don't you or Ernie do it? Not me. Never."

He looked down at the table. Ernie put one hand over his eyes. Henry looked around the table, from face to face.

Lucas let the silence accumulate.

Then he said, "If you like, I'll make the offer to her."

Billy looked up at him.

"You?"

"She invited me to dinner next week. Tuesday. I could do it then. If I get the chance."

He finished his beer.

Ernie had uncovered his eyes and was studying Lucas's face, as if it were the map of a newly discovered planet.

"I told you I was her new toy. She's curious about me. I don't mind talking to her about it. I'll try to make her think it's her idea."

"You're not getting any of the money, you understand?" Ernie whispered. "You understand?"

"I do."

"Maybe you want to cut your own deal," Billy said.

"I don't. I told you, I've got all the money I need."

"Nobody has all the money they need."

"If you don't want me to help, that's fine with me."

Billy looked at Ernie and Henry.

"Let him try," Ernie said.

"Let him." (That was Henry.)

Billy didn't want to agree, but he did.

"I think I'll have another beer," Lucas said.

7

The Next Town

On Thursday evening Lucas drove to Margot's house. It was a misty, windless day.

He was pleased. Henry, Billy and Ernie might not like him or trust him. But they were beginning to believe they needed him.

Emily just wanted to solve the mystery of Lucas. He wouldn't make it easy for her.

Fay was primed for falling in love with him. Every morning, in the Cascades, he could see that she felt freer, more confident, more a part of his life.

Margot wasn't part of the plan. He had to be careful with her: he always seemed to be answering questions she hadn't asked. And, too often, he told her the truth.

But she lives in the next town, far away. Far, far away.

When she answered the door, he leaned forward and kissed her cheek, and followed her into the house. He handed her a bottle of Merlot, wrapped in foil and decorated with a ribbon bow.

She said, "Dinner is still simmering. I'll open this and we can have a drink first."

He nodded.

The house had a small center hall with steps leading up to the second floor. On the right was an open double door to the dining room, which was separated from the kitchen by a waist-high wall, topped with slatted, wooden shutters. The shutters were open and he could see the kitchen beyond them. On the left of the hall was the living room. A comfortable looking couch and two large upholstered chairs faced a fireplace in the far wall. Crowded bookshelves occupied the two walls in the nearest corner of the room. Paintings and photographs were hung serendipitously.

It seemed like a home that was at ease with itself.

"The living room's to your left," Margot said. "Make yourself comfortable. I'll join you in a minute. There's cheese and crackers and some fruit on the coffee table."

He sat on the couch and waited for her, contemplating a wedge of Jarlsburg and another of brie on the cutting board. A ceramic dish held clusters of red and green grapes. And a small bowl was filled with mixed nuts. He sampled a handful.

When she came in, Margot was carrying the opened bottle of Merlot and two crystal goblets. She settled herself next to Lucas on the couch. He could smell a faint aura of perfume, a distant hint of flowers.

He leaned forward and breathed in her scent.

"I thought you're allergic to flowers."

"I am. But it's the pollen that bothers me, not the smell of the flowers."

She poured a glass of wine for each of them.

"I'm a little nervous," she confessed, "I hope I didn't ruin the coq au vin."

He touched his glass to hers. "Don't be nervous. I'm not judging you."

She smiled and sipped some wine.

I'm not judging you.

He tasted the wine.

"How's that challenging job of yours?" she asked.

"I've already been promoted."

"What talent! From rags to riches in four days."

"Well, I'm not exactly the CEO."

"What exactly are you?"

He smiled.

"I guess I'm a consultant."

"I wish I knew what you were talking about. I don't suppose you'd like to explain why you're smiling."

"Not right now."

He leaned forward and she turned her face toward him. He kissed her mouth gently, pulled away, then leaned forward and kissed her again, in the same way.

His feelings surprised him: his hunger for women had always been aggressive; now, for the first time, he seemed to feel both passion and tenderness.

"You're a very confusing man. In the middle of shutting me out, you come closer to me."

"Pennington has nothing to do with you. This is a different world. A different universe."

"If you say so."

"What about your job search?"

"I've lined up some interviews over the next couple of weeks. Two brokers and a research group. There are lots of jobs out there."

Lucas reached for some grapes. He watched her slice off a sliver of brie and spread it on a cracker.

"It'll be great to get back to real work again," she said. "I've been reviewing some of the reports I did, white papers, some studies. They're pretty good, if I may be immodest for a moment."

"You may."

"You came along just in time."

"Me?"

"I don't like to admit it, but you're the reason I'm doing this. I've been stuck in the same groove for too long. I've been doing things by rote. When you live alone, there's a funny kind of inertia that can creep up on you. Have you noticed that? You're eating the same muffin every morning, following the same routine, saying the same things, even thinking the same things. The small pleasures are comforting, but there are no big pleasures."

She put her hand on his knee. It was so light, he could hardly feel it.

"Then someone makes you remember that you shouldn't settle for small pleasures."

"Margot, you don't really know me."

"It isn't a question of how well I know you. What matters is that I want to be more, to do more. I want to go back to work and knock 'em dead. Then I want to tell you all about it, so you'll be proud of me."

"I'm looking forward to that."

She stood up. "I'd better get back to the kitchen. The timer's about to go off."

He stood up, too, and put his arms around her waist. She pressed herself against him and reached up, circling his neck with her arms. He felt the small, soft hills of her breasts and her belly against him. She kissed his mouth. Her lips parted and she pressed her tongue against his.

She felt slender and strong in his arms.

They heard the ping-ping-ping of the timer.

She leaned back, away from him.

"That's dinner."

After the first taste, Lucas sighed.

"Delicious. An old family recipe?"

"As a matter of fact, yes. My mother's a great cook. But whenever I asked her how she made something, she was always vague. She'd say, 'A little of this, a touch of that, a pinch of this.' And I would say, How much is 'a little'? How many teaspoons in 'a touch'? When I got married, she finally came clean: she gave me a notebook filled with her handwritten recipes."

"You always get along well with your folks?"

"Yes, once I understood what to expect from them. My father is very emotional, but he's not comfortable showing it. He never told me he thought I looked pretty, or that I was smart. He never even told me or my brother that he loved us. But he told those things to my mother—and she told us. Then I realized that he was the one with the problem, not me. Mom was always easier to love. But I thought she gave in to him too much. I always wanted her to be stronger, to stand up for herself. Maybe she got her way more than I thought she did. Anyway, we get along fine. What about you?"

He hesitated (*the N.S.A. pause*, he thought). "My father was never home much. He was a sales rep for a publishing company. Spent most of the year on the road, visiting customers, working at book fairs, trade shows. When he was home, he was always tired. Slept a lot. Did paperwork for the office. He died when I was eleven or twelve. I hardly noticed that he was gone. While he was alive, my mother wasn't a happy camper and she let me know it. After he died, she was worse. She dated a little, but not for long. She never got married again. And she started talking about him like he was a great guy. He left her a big chunk of insurance: maybe that's what she loved about him."

"Do you have any brothers or sisters?"

"No. I'd like another glass of wine."

As she refilled his glass she smiled warmly and said, "Thank you for telling me, Luke."

"How do you know it's the truth?"

She kissed his cheek.

"Thank you," she repeated. "Would you like some more chicken? Some potatoes?"

"More of both."

After dinner, Margot said, "There's an old-fashioned ice cream parlor not far from here. It's a nice walk, past a little lake and through the park. We can have dessert and coffee there, if you like."

"Sounds good."

Outside, the mist softened the outlines of the houses, the trees, the street lamps, the moon. They walked slowly. He shortened his stride to match her small steps. He reached for her hand and held it close to his side. As they walked, she moved closer to him, until her fingers brushed against him, and his fingers against her.

They were silent for a time. Lucas shut away all the people in Pennington, his plans for them, his past, his future. He held Margot's small hand firmly, gently, as if it would die if he held it too tightly, or fly away if he held it too loosely.

After five or six blocks, they came to the lake, a narrow patch of water surrounded by a border of trees, open lawns and a scattering of park benches.

"We call it a lake," Margot said, "but it's more like a very big puddle. It's a nice place to sit on a Sunday morning and read the paper."

"Feel like sitting here for a few minutes?"

"Ummm. Over there."

With a nod, she motioned to an unoccupied bench. They watched tissues of mist, shimmering with moonlight, drift over the lake. The raucous voice of a crow emerged from the darkness. A

transistor radio somewhere across the lake sang a song in Spanish.

She rested her hand on his thigh, her fingers curled lightly around it. He covered her hand with his.

"This is one of those times when everything seems just right," she said. "To me, at least. Maybe it's the Catholic in me, but all of this can't be an accident, can it?"

"Why not? Think of all the bad times. All the mistakes. All the suffering. Is that also part of the plan?"

"I guess I can't answer that."

"Neither can I. What if it's all just accidental? Random chance?"

"That may be true, whether I like it or not."

He smiled. "I want the world to be what you want it to be. So, from now on, everything makes sense. Okay?"

She leaned her head against his shoulder.

"That is one noisy crow," he laughed.

"He's saying, 'Margot is very glad—caw! caw! caw!—that she met Luke.'"

"So you speak crow, eh? I wonder if that bird knows why Margot is so glad. Luke hasn't made it easy for her."

The crow continued his soliloquy.

She listened for a moment. "The crow says, 'She feels how strong he is. And she also feels—that he's afraid.'"

"Afraid?"

She looked up at him and nodded.

"It doesn't matter what it is. It doesn't matter if you tell me. But I won't run away from it, whatever it is."

"Are you ready for dessert? I know I am."

She stood up, leaned over and kissed his mouth lightly.

"Me, too."

The ice cream parlor was almost empty. An elderly couple sat at one table, and a trio of noisy teenage girls at another.

Lucas ordered a double scoop of coffee ice cream. Margot ordered a hot fudge sundae. They sat at a table by the window, looking out at the quiet, Thursday-night street.

"I used to take my dates to the local ice cream parlor. And it looked a lot like this. I feel like the oldest high school kid in the world."

"That's a new kind of smile for you, Luke."

"Is it?"

"I think I can actually see the high school kid in you."

He looked at his reflection in the window glass.

"You may be right."

He turned away from the window and added, "But that was a thousand years ago."

"I'll bet you were a big shot in high school. And college, too. You were handsome and smart. Probably played on one of the varsity teams. And, of course, the ladies loved you."

"What about you?"

"Nobody noticed me. I was one of the nerds in the Math Club. Didn't date much. And I didn't mind, either. I wasn't interested in being a kid. It was a waste of time. I wanted to be a grownup right away."

"So you left college to get married?"

"Even a nerd can be a romantic idiot. John, my husband, was very charming. He talked a good game. All of a sudden, I was somebody else."

Margot pointed her finger at Lucas. "I thought we were talking about you."

"Were we?"

"Do you want to stay over, tonight?"

She's hearing love songs. Step back.

He smiled.

"Weren't you the one who said that sex isn't that great?"

100

"I guess I did." She laughed. "I didn't think you were listening."

"I was."

"Should I have waited for you to ask me?"

He reached out, pulled her hand toward him and kissed it lightly.

"No, that has nothing to do with it."

"Then, why not?"

He caressed her hand.

"I don't know how long I'm going to stay in Pennington."

"I don't care how long you'll be here. No, that's not true. I do care. But you're with me right now. Stay with me."

"Give it time."

"Okay," she whispered.

They didn't speak on the walk back to her house. She linked her arm in his and leaned against him. The streets were empty. The mist was thicker and wetter. The air heavy and warm.

At her front door, she turned the key and opened it.

"Would you like something to drink? Coffee, maybe?"

"No, thanks."

After a few beats, she asked, "Is there anything special you'd like to do on Saturday night?"

"Is there a movie around that you're interested in? Anything you want to do is fine with me."

She kissed his mouth.

"Anything you want to do is fine with me."

"That sounds familiar."

He thought of Fay, of the way it would be with her. And tonight suddenly became more distant.

He didn't live in Fulton with Margot Sinclair. He lived in Pennington. With Fay and Emily Schuyler Grant. And the wind chimes that played their songs for no one.

Things in Pennington were beginning to fall into place. And that's where he lived.

He kissed her hair. "See you on Saturday night."

8

Fay

Henry wasn't there when he reported to work on Friday. Leo told Lucas to continue cleaning the shed, and asked Billy Miles, Jr., to help. But Billy said he had strained his back, so he wouldn't be able to do much. Leo told Billy to go home early.

On Saturday morning, the nursery was unexpectedly busy. Henry wasn't there. Billy Jr. called in sick. So Lucas helped Leo with the customers, loading purchases into cars and trucks, and even making a couple of sales.

That night Margot was quiet, as if she were afraid of saying the wrong thing, or making the wrong move. They had dinner at a steak house and saw a romantic movie.

He wanted to comfort her, but didn't. He kissed her goodnight and told her he'd call during the week.

He wondered if Margot had told Jill she was seeing him. It wasn't likely. But if Jill knew, Joey would know, too. And so would Fay, eventually.

Fay. She watched him now with gentler eyes. She smiled at

him wistfully, as if they shared some secret memory. She was ready. He only had to reach out for her.

She reminded him of what he had been. He had seen those eyes and that smile so many times. He had danced that same dance so many times: a touch, a whisper, a kiss, a sudden spasm of pleasure, an aftertaste of disgust.

He had never touched Fay, and yet he was already sated with her.

It was raining on Sunday morning, so Lucas didn't go to the Cascades. He welcomed a few hours alone.

It was still raining in the afternoon, when he knocked on Fay's front door.

She laughed when she saw him and asked, "Why didn't you just come upstairs?"

"This is a formal date, so I thought I would act accordingly."

She liked that. He knew she would.

"Do you know how to get to Exeter?"

"No. You'll have to be my navigator."

"The college is on Forty-Six A. That's a spur that splits off from the main road a few miles east of Fulton. It can't take more than a half hour to get there, so we've got plenty of time."

On the way to his car, she shielded them both with her umbrella.

As he drove through the warm rain, the windshield wipers punctuated their conversation with a rigid, insistent rhythm.

"I'm sorry I missed our morning run today," he said.

"I am, too. I'll make up for it tomorrow. I promise."

"One of these days, we'll run all the way to Fulton."

"I'm not aiming quite that high."

"Look how far you've come already."

Her voice softened. "I'm really enjoying it. I'm grateful to you."

He ignored the intimacy.

"My pleasure."

She paused and the steady beat of the wiper blades filled in the silence.

"How's the job going?"

"Fine. No complaints."

"Is Henry harassing you much?"

"No. We're getting along pretty well."

"You haven't been to one of his Bible classes, I hope."

"Not yet."

"I've heard they're not really classes. They're prayer meetings. Still planning to go?"

"I'm curious."

"I can't imagine why. He's not worth the effort."

"I like to find out things for myself."

"Be my guest."

Lucas let the sound of the blades finish that topic and introduce a new one.

"I've been wondering, Fay, why you've stayed here. I know: this is your home town, et cetera, et cetera. But there must be more to it than that."

"There isn't. You should understand. You lived in New York. But you came here because it reminds you of home, right?"

"Right."

"Well, this is my home. It's as simple as that."

He nodded.

She apparently felt she had to reinforce what she'd just said. "I'm not a complicated person. I wanted to live in Pennington, so I came back."

"But it's not exactly a great place for a single woman."

She laughed. "You've noticed."

"Maybe the choices looked better a few years ago."

"Twenty years ago."

"Did you come back for someone?"

The windshield wipers clicked back and forth several times before she said, "Yes. But that's very old news. It doesn't matter now."

He wondered how much it had mattered, and who it had been.

"For someone who never says much about himself, you're quite a detective."

He nodded and smiled.

He said, "It's your turn. Give me the third degree. I'll tell all."

"Hmmm. Okay. Were you ever married?"

"No. I was engaged a couple of times. But I was too restless. I would have been a lousy husband."

"What company did you work for?"

"Computer Systems & Technologies. It's a consulting firm that also sells software."

"I can't picture you doing that kind of work."

"Why not?"

"I don't know. You're just not the type."

"I'm glad my customers didn't feel that way."

"Why did you retire? You're only about fifty, right?"

"Fifty-three. I retired because the company was sold. New management came in. They decided to bring in their own salespeople. And they made a very good early retirement offer. Too good to pass up."

"And you didn't consider going to work for another company?"

"I made some half-hearted efforts to find another job. But it didn't take much to discourage me. I've been on the road for a while. Almost a year now. Looking for a new home."

"This is not exactly a great place for a single man."

"I guess you haven't met my landlady."

He turned to glance at her. She was smiling as if he had just kissed her for the first time.

The windshield wipers hummed and clicked.

After a long pause, she said, "I haven't thought much about dating for a few years. A few years. That sounds terrible, doesn't it?"

"No. We're not teen-agers. Why go out with someone just for the sake of going out?"

"Yes, that's exactly how I feel. It's hard to believe that Joey and I grew up in the same family, isn't it?"

They were driving through Fulton now.

Fay added, "Joey tells me you're the talk of the town these days. What's going on?"

"It's no big thing."

"That's not what I hear. He tells me that you're helping Billy and Ernie on some kind of deal for the old factory. Joey says you've got an in with Emily Grant."

"He's exaggerating. I haven't even spoken to her about it yet."

"How did you get involved?"

"It's a long story."

"Joey said Emily invited you to the Grange for dinner."

"That's true."

"Why would she do that?"

"This is a small town. With a small cast of characters. She's bored. And I'm somebody new. Someone who isn't afraid of her. She met me when I was working at the Grange with Henry."

"But, why . . . ?"

"Fay. It isn't important. Nothing may come of it. Let's just enjoy today, huh?"

❦

The audience for *Alexander Nevsky* was a mix of students and teachers, who seemed to regard the film with religious solemnity. Lucas thought that the movie was static and pretentious. He had always been impatient with the rituals of fiction, and he was scornful of fiction's trappings—metaphor, symbolism, imagery.

If you know the truth, tell me what it is. Don't make me guess. If you don't know the truth, don't waste my time.

He watched the flickering images on the screen, listened to the music, read the titles and, when Fay looked at him, acted as if he was enjoying himself.

When the film ended, he applauded as enthusiastically as anyone else.

"Beautiful," Fay said. "Better than I remember."

"Yes, it is. Now, may I ask a practical question?"

"Sure."

"Where would you like to eat?"

"There's a place right on Forty-Six in Fulton. In fact, it's called Route Forty-Six. The food's pretty good."

It was still raining and, on the way to the car, he held the umbrella and put his arm around her waist to pull her closer. It was the first time he had touched her.

On the drive to the restaurant, she said, "I can't imagine anyone else in town who would be interested in *Alexander Nevsky*. You really performed a public service today."

"I just wanted to do something I thought you'd enjoy."

"And I appreciate it."

He smiled at her.

She said, "It's kind of a gloomy day, huh?"

"Perfect for Russian movies."

She laughed.

"When we get back," she said, "if you like, we can sit by the fireplace and listen to music and drink some wine."

"A fire in the summertime? Why not? That sounds perfect, as long as we don't sit too close to it."

She laughed. "We'll make believe there's a fire. It's just a nice place to sit."

"What about Joey?"

"He went away for the weekend with God Knows Who."

"I think I met her."

She laughed again.

At dinner, he was reserved, but he spoke to her more affectionately and more seriously.

She became more tentative.

When they were drinking their coffee, he reached out for her hand. She hesitated for a moment, then yielded. He sensed that her hesitation was instinctive: she was afraid of what he might be, or what he might do. But when he touched her fingers, she responded as if that no longer mattered.

They drove back to Pennington without much conversation. When they arrived, Fay opened a chilled bottle of Chardonnay and picked some CDs—romantic ballads by Frank Sinatra, Barbra Streisand and Tony Bennett.

They slipped off their shoes and sat on the floor near the fireplace, their backs against the couch. Lucas put his arm around Fay's shoulder, as they sipped their wine.

He took a deep breath, put down his wine glass, took hers and put it alongside his. He touched her face with his hand, stroked her hair, then leaned forward and kissed her mouth. She pressed her

lips to his and tasted his mouth with her tongue.

He felt her breast, her hip, the long, firm muscles of her thigh. He let the wine and the music and her flesh lead him into familiar patterns, familiar places.

As she took off her clothes, she became less spirited, more fragile. Naked, she was awkward and shy. Her narrow hips and small breasts and long, muscular legs gave her an ambiguous sexual appearance.

He followed the ritual, said the words, reassured her ("I'm using a condom"), gave her pleasure, gave himself pleasure.

Afterwards, when he was holding her in his arms, her head resting on his chest, her hands caressing his body, he wondered if it would be different with Margot. Would it matter that he cared about her? Or would he fall into the same mechanical routine?

Fay kissed his chest, murmured something.

He should have been pleased. Fay was ready now. But all he felt was a familiar sense of disgust.

On Monday, Henry was at the garden center when Lucas arrived.

"I think you can finish the shed today, right?" Leo said.

"Maybe someone else can do that," Henry said.

"No, let me take care of it. It's almost done."

Henry shrugged. He was uneasy.

Lucas decided to add to his uneasiness.

"Henry, I've been thinking about dropping in on one of your Bible study classes."

Leo was surprised.

Henry studied Lucas suspiciously.

"Is that so?"

"Sure. I don't know much about religion, but I'm always open to new ideas. When's the next class?"

"I haven't set a date yet. Next week, sometime. I'll let you know."

"Good."

There was only one waist-high pile of trash left in the shed, in a far corner. Lucas attacked it methodically, loaded the wheelbarrow, dumped it into the pit, and returned for more.

Lucas knew Henry was comfortable with primary colors, black and white, good and evil. And, for him, that's all there was.

But he can't be sure about me. And he hates to be unsure.

It took three wheelbarrow loads to empty the shed. After the final load, Lucas took a breather for a few minutes. He walked around the pit and into the stand of trees behind it on the edge of the Cascades. He kept going deeper into the woods, clearing his lungs of the musty odors of the shed, breathing the clean summer air.

At the rim of a little clearing, he stopped suddenly and shivered with fear. He looked up at a stiff, angular bush that was at least two or three feet taller than he was. The lower branches were thick and woody and covered with brown thorns. The new shoots were purplish, with small, dark green leaves and tiny white, four-petalled flowers. The new branches were covered with large, cherry-red thorns—thorns that were attached to the branches by translucent, bloody membranes.

Lucas closed his eyes and turned away. He breathed deeply, trying to calm himself. He looked at the bush again.

This isn't my dream.

The bloody thorns, reaching over his head, reaching for the sky, caught the sunlight and glowed red.

Lucas touched the woody, old-growth branches of the bush. He felt their reality.

This isn't my dream.

He returned to the garden center. Henry was in the office at the back of the building, reading catalogues.

Lucas knocked on the open door and Henry motioned him in.

"I just finished cleaning the shed."

"Okay."

"I want to ask you about a bush I saw in the woods. Just past the pit."

"What about it?"

"It was maybe eight or ten feet tall. Thick, woody branches. Very small white flowers. But the new growth was purple. And it had thorns with red membranes attached to them. Do you know what I'm talking about?"

"That's a wild rose—a Wingthorn Rose. You don't see many of them around here."

"A rose? With white flowers?"

"Roses come in all kinds of colors. Live and learn."

"I guess."

Henry leaned back in his chair, waited a beat, and then said, "Ready for your meeting with Emily tomorrow?"

Lucas nodded.

"Yes. And I'm sure she's ready for me, too."

"She's ready for anything," Henry laughed.

"What's next on my work schedule?"

"Go help Leo at the counter. You've got to save your energy."

Henry laughed again.

Lucas smiled and left the office.

He tried to think of Emily Grant. He tried to think of Fay. He even tried to think of Margot.

But all he could think of was the Wingthorn Rose.

9

Jeanette

The front door of the Grange was a massive slab of dark oak, covered with intricate carvings of flowers and birds. The knocker was bronze: a huge, highly polished, rococo "S" with the name "Schuyler" etched along its length. An illuminated brass button on the door frame suggested a quieter alternative: the doorbell.

Lucas chose the harsher pounding of the knocker: once, twice, three times.

The door was answered by an elderly male servant dressed in a white shirt, black tie, and black suit that was slightly shiny from years of wear.

"Good evening. I'm Lucas Murdoch."

"Good evening, Mr. Murdoch. Please come in. I'm Cameron."

"Nice to meet you, Cameron."

The front door opened onto a broad foyer. A short flight of steps at the opposite end of the foyer led up to a very large, high-ceilinged hallway lit by three massive chandeliers, with several doors on either side of it, and a carpeted, winding staircase at its center.

"Mrs. Grant asked me to show you to the library. She'll join you there."

Lucas followed Cameron out of the foyer and to the left, through an open door and into a brightly lit room with two levels of crowded bookshelves on three of its four walls. A fireplace was set into the fourth wall. An oil portrait of a gloomy young man hung over it and three color photographs stared out from the mantle piece. A rectangular oak table, surrounded by four chairs, stood near the fireplace. On the table were a tray of hors d'oeuvres, two wine bottles, a stack of circular leather coasters and some glasses.

Cameron asked, "Would you like a glass of wine while you wait, sir? A Chardonnay? Cabernet sauvignon? Or would you prefer a cocktail?"

"Cabernet would be fine, thank you."

Cameron poured the wine and handed the glass to Lucas. He separated a coaster from the stack and put it on the table.

Deftly, silently, he picked up the tray of hors d'oeuvres and offered it to Lucas.

"No, thank you."

With a slight nod of his head, Cameron replaced the tray on the table and said, "Mrs. Grant should be down in a few minutes."

After he left, Lucas walked over to the fireplace to get a closer look at the photographs. One showed a young couple sitting on the grass near a flower bed on a bright, summer day. The man's smile was forced and uncomfortable. The woman, who was holding an infant in her arms, seemed relaxed and contented.

A larger photo, of a two- or three-year-old girl, dominated the center of the mantle piece. Lucas assumed that this was the infant a few years later. Her face was fine-boned and angular. Her

eyes watched the camera lens without expression, opaquely. She was almost smiling.

The third picture was Emily Schuyler Grant in a formal, seated pose, the chair at an angle to the camera. She was smiling regally, her face turned toward the camera. Standing behind, with one hand resting on her shoulder, was the little girl, ten or eleven years old, her eyes still opaque, the ghost of a smile still on her lips.

"Good evening, Mr. Murdoch."

"Good evening, Mrs. Grant."

Emily was accompanied by a tall, slender, teen-age replica of the girl in the photographs, whose face had become more attractive, whose eyes still shielded her thoughts, whose mouth still hinted at a smile.

Both women wore long, pastel, summery dresses. Emily had fastened a small, pink jeweled flower in her hair, and wore a glittering flower necklace and earrings to match. The girl wore much quieter jewelry: tiny diamond earrings and a delicate diamond necklace.

"Mr. Murdoch, Lucas, this is my granddaughter, Jeanette Grant."

Lucas shook the young woman's hand. "It's a pleasure to meet you, Jeanette."

"My pleasure, Mr. Murdoch," she said, though she didn't sound pleased.

Her voice echoed Emily's: throaty and resonant.

Emily and Jeanette sat down at the table, and Emily motioned for Lucas to join them.

He sat opposite them.

"Now, would you pour a glass of the Cabernet for each of us, please?" Emily asked. "Thank you."

"Meeting in the library. That's a nice touch."

"I'm just trying to provide you with a subtle tour of Schuyler Grange. You've already seen the greenhouse, the grounds and the game room. Now the library. Soon, the dining room. And, after dinner, I'll show you the conservatory."

Lucas smiled.

"This was my husband's favorite place. He read a great deal, mostly novels. I never could understand that. My son, Jeanette's father, was cut from the same mold."

"Grandmother is a pragmatist," Jeanette said. "She can't abide fiction. But I tend to find truth a little boring. Which camp are you in, Mr. Murdoch?"

"Your grandmother's."

"Alas."

After a long, thoughtful sip of wine, Emily said, "I like the way you look in a dark blue suit."

"Thank you." He turned to her granddaughter. "How old are you, Jeanette?"

"Fifteen, and counting."

"Impatient to grow up?"

"I don't like being between things."

"Where do you go to school?"

"I don't. I've had tutors all my life. They've done wonders with me. I speak French and German. I can read Latin and Greek. Just imagine how I show off at parties."

She plucked an hors d'oeuvre from the tray, ate it and drank some wine.

Lucas asked, "Do you regret not going to school with other kids?"

"No. I don't get along very well with people. Especially young people. Besides, Grandmother wants to make sure that I get the best possible education and she doesn't trust any school to give me that. Someday soon, I think she's going to buy me my own

university. I am her only significant heir, you know. All she has is me and her roses."

Lucas was impressed with the way someone as young as Jeanette could manage to sound truthful and satirical at the same time.

"So you're never lonely?"

"Never," Jeanette said, and added, "Grandmother tells me that you enjoy being enigmatic."

"I'm not really an enigma. Just a stranger."

Jeanette almost allowed her smile to escape.

She said, "Camus would say that we are all strangers—to each other. Because we are always alone when we die."

"I read Camus when I was in college, but I must admit that all I can remember is how to pronounce his name."

"I could pronounce Camus when I was only eight years old."

"As you can see, my granddaughter is a rather serious young woman."

Jeanette nodded in agreement.

Her movements seemed carefully controlled and choreographed, as if she were following a prescribed routine. He couldn't see beyond the veil of her eyes. Her distant smile was like a garbled message, impossible to read, impossible to decode. He thought he sensed anger, but her face was a smooth mask of serenity.

Despite what Jeanette said, Lucas didn't feel any tension between the two women. It was as if Emily and she were playing a scene they had played a hundred times before, a scene that, with repetition, had lost its emotional content.

He watched them sitting stiffly, side by side, and thought, *Maybe I've found the key to Emily's door.*

That discovery should have pleased him, but it only made him uneasy.

He thought of what Emily had said about never loving anyone. And then he thought of his daughter's face, her smile, her eyes.

"Have you learned anything about flowers yet?" Emily asked.

"A little."

"But you're not in Pennington to smell the flowers, are you, Mr. Murdoch?"

"I don't mind smelling them, Mrs. Grant. I just can't tell one from another."

Jeanette laughed. "Bravo, Mr. Murdoch. You know, for Grandmother, flowers are the ideal companions. The *first* thing you do is bury them."

"Jeanette," Emily said, with a touch of weariness.

Jeanette took another hors d'oeuvre and a long, slow sip of wine.

"Where did you say you worked, when you lived in New York?" Emily asked.

"Mrs. Grant . . ."

"Call me Emily."

"All right, Emily. I'd rather not say. If you know all about me, I won't seem nearly so interesting any more, and you'll never invite me to dinner again."

"I have a feeling that if I knew all about you, you'd be even more interesting. But I can be patient."

Lucas gestured toward the painting over the mantel piece.

"Is that one of your Schuyler ancestors?"

"Yes. My great-grandfather, Jan Schuyler. He's the one who founded the company. He could see how fast things were moving— away from farming and toward manufacturing. He got in on the ground floor, built our first factory—not here, but in Hartford. It was my father who moved most of the operation to Pennington, closer to

home. We still have a Hartford headquarters, but the Management Committee meets here, of course."

"You're the sole owner of the company?"

"I am."

"No SEC. No annual reports. No shareowners to worry about. That makes doing business a lot easier, doesn't it?"

"I wouldn't have it any other way. I have all the votes. I make all the decisions. And neither the government nor anyone else has anything to say about it."

"I guess your husband didn't have much of a role in running the business?"

Emily smiled. "He didn't have any role at all. My company is a Schuyler company. Unfortunately, I was my father's only child. I couldn't carry on the name, but I'm still a Schuyler. I wish my son had been a Schuyler, too. But he wasn't. Not in any way."

"Grandmother didn't think much of my father, or my mother, for that matter. Grandmother has another child, you know—a daughter, who lives in California: Aunt Julie. But she's even lower on the scale than Father was: she never cared about money or the business or Grandmother, either. She left home when she was twenty and never looked back. She's been married, or sort of married, several times. She has a few children, but we've never seen them. She's mentioned in the will, but she won't get much. I'm the big winner."

"So you're going to take over the company someday?"

Jeanette nodded and smiled.

"I can't wait to fire people. I'll do it on Christmas Eve, I think."

She laughed and, surprisingly, it was a soft, self-deprecating laugh.

"How old were you when you lost your parents?" Lucas asked.

"They were killed in a plane crash. They were on the family plane, on vacation, and it went down in the Rocky Mountains somewhere. I was two years old. If there weren't photographs, I wouldn't remember them at all."

"That must have been difficult."

Jeanette sipped her wine and said, "But I had Grandmother," and there was no way to tell what she really meant by that.

Dinner was served in a high-ceilinged, dimly lit room that Emily called the family dining room. The table could have accommodated twenty people.

"The dining hall is much bigger," Emily said. "When I was young, we had huge gatherings there virtually every week. My mother loved being a hostess. I can't imagine why. I remember the crowds of hangers-on. The noise, the clutter, the waste of time and money. When Mother died, that was the end of it. My father had more important things to do. And so do I."

"I guess I should be even more flattered by your dinner invitation."

Emily smiled.

"You should be."

"She'll get tired of you, sooner or later, Mr. Murdoch. When she's figured you out."

"I know. You can see why I'm so intent on being mysterious."

After a long pause, Emily said, "Perhaps the mystery has something to do with my factory."

Lucas tried to look puzzled. "Why do you think so?"

"I'm told that you've been meeting with Billy and Ernie and Henry."

Who told her?

"Meeting? That's a very formal way of putting it. I run into them at Sarge's Diner once in a while."

"Surely they've tried to enlist you in their little army."

"Why would they? I'm an outsider."

"But I've taken an interest in you. Doesn't that make you a desirable ally?"

"They don't trust me, Emily. Why should they?"

"Why should I?"

"This is getting better by the minute," Jeanette said. "Do you mind if I take notes? For my memoirs?"

"I've heard about the shopping-mall proposal from them—and from you, too," Lucas said. "But I'm just an observer."

"And what is your considered opinion, as an observer?"

"I'm not sure I have an opinion."

Emily shook her head.

"Of course you do."

Lucas chewed a mouthful of food slowly, thoughtfully.

Jeanette said, "The suspense is killing us," and laughed.

Lucas smiled. "You can probably make the shopping mall work for you, if you look at it in the right way."

"And what way is the right way?"

"The factory is just a dead zone now, isn't it?"

"Yes."

"Next door, in Fulton, there are plenty of stores—and people from this town and others around here spend a lot of money in those stores. Money that could be spent in Pennington."

"That's fine with me."

Lucas smiled again. "It could be finer."

Jeanette said, "Mr. Murdoch, that was an evil smile if I ever saw one."

Emily's self-proclaimed patience was fading.

"Go on, Lucas."

"Why not sell the factory property to developers—for a shopping mall. But with conditions. You keep a big percentage of it for yourself. You put your name on it—*Schuyler*, of course. And you run one of the anchor stores."

"We're not retailers. We never were."

"I know that. But it might be handy to have one location—in one small town in Connecticut—where you do some test marketing. You wouldn't actually be competing with any of your retailers. And you could get some real-time feedback on new products—new sales approaches—without any risk."

"And what about the Three Musketeers? Why should I do anything that will profit them?"

"Picture it, Emily. The Schuyler factory used to be the magnet at the center of this town. The profit center. And now it will be the Schuyler Mall. Your mall. Your name. Your profit center. Sure, Billy and Ernie and Henry will get a finder's fee. But, if you're deciding on the terms of the deal, you can probably see to it that they don't get much."

It was Emily's turn to smile.

"What's your cut going to be?"

"I told them that, if a deal goes through, I didn't want a penny from them. And I don't want anything from you, either."

"They didn't believe you, of course. And neither do I."

"I don't need the money. I'm living just the way I want to live."

Emily and Jeanette watched him for a few silent moments, as if they were waiting for a time-bomb to explode. Lucas took a few bites of food and sipped his wine.

At last, Emily asked, "You're enjoying all of this, aren't you?"

"All of what?"

"Appearing mysteriously, out of nowhere," she said, too

dramatically, satirizing what she really felt, "descending on a small town and making things happen."

Lucas laughed. "Okay, okay. I'll tell you what I'll do, even though it's going to spoil some of the fun. I'll solve the mystery of Lucas Murdoch."

Jeanette leaned forward and asked, "Is there a murder involved?"

"Not quite. Ladies, in my previous life—in New York City—I was a software salesman. I was relatively successful. Lived comfortably. Never married. Traveled extensively. And when the company was bought by another, I was asked to retire early with a decent pension, which I did. And because I grew up in a small town in Pennsylvania, I decided to try small-town living again. That's what I'm doing in Pennington. That's all I'm doing."

Neither Emily nor Jeanette said a word.

"Disappointing, huh?"

"No," Emily said, flatly, neutrally.

"I liked you better when you were mysterious," Jeanette said.

For a moment, he could see beyond the veil that shielded her eyes. Her half-smile almost seemed like a warning.

10

The Factory Conversion Committee

On Wednesday night, after dinner, Lucas attended a meeting of the Factory Conversion Committee, chaired by First Selectman Billy Miles. The other members of the committee were Ernie; Henry, who had invited Lucas; Don Appleby, who ran the general store with his sister Laura; and Luther Avedon, the Chief of Police.

It was a private meeting in a long, narrow conference room on the second floor of the Town Hall. Lucas was careful to arrive almost half an hour late.

"I lost track of the time," he explained.

"Sit down, sit down," Billy said.

It was a warm, sticky night. Billy's head glowed with a sheen of sweat.

"Lucas, I've filled everybody in, about your conversation with Mrs. Grant," Henry said. "So you can bring us up to date."

Luther interrupted, "I still don't get it. Did you make her some kind of offer?"

He looked around the room and asked, "We didn't decide on any offer, did we?"

He was a lean, angry little man. Lucas had met him at Sarge's Diner a couple of times.

He has the look of someone who welcomes anger. Who feeds on anger.

Billy tapped a nervous rhythm on the table top. "No, no, no, Luther. Nothing like that."

Luther wasn't pleased. "This is supposed to be a committee. We're supposed to be making decisions together. What're Don and me? Window dressing?"

Don Appleby nodded in agreement, but didn't say anything. He was a somber thirty-year-old, with deep-set, dark brown eyes, a long, straight nose, and a comically small chin. Lucas wondered if he knew how to smile.

Billy tried to soothe Luther's nerves. "No one's made any decisions, none at all."

Henry held his hand out in front of him, palm toward Luther, as if he were trying to stop a speeding car.

"We were getting nowhere with Emily," he said. "You know that. Time is running out, and Lucas seemed to catch her eye. We were just trying to find another way to reach her."

"Why the hell would she listen to him?"

Now Henry was getting angry, too.

"*We* don't have much of a track record, do we? It was worth a try."

Luther's eyes flickered around the table, reminding everyone that he wasn't satisfied.

Then he sat back in his chair, concentrated on Lucas and said, "Go ahead."

"I was just exploring some possibilities with her. Informally."

"What possibilities?" Luther asked.

Lucas motioned toward Billy. "I'd been told that she had no

intention of selling the factory. The first time I met her, she said as much. But for someone like me, who's spent his life as a salesman, she was a challenge. And I thought that as an outsider, as someone who doesn't have a history with her, I could test the waters—maybe find out what it would take to make her reconsider."

Billy's fingers kept up a soft drumbeat.

Lucas continued, "The question really is: What do you offer somebody who has already won the game?"

He let the question float in the air for a moment.

Then he said, "You don't fight her. You flatter her, so she can feel even more like a winner."

Luther leaned forward across the table, pointed his finger at Lucas, and asked, "What the hell does that mean?"

"It isn't that Emily would mind making more money, but she'd like a little bonus along with it. The chance to rub your faces in it."

Ernie spoke for the first time.

"Again," he whispered.

"So I made a couple of suggestions to her. I said that she could sell the property, but not all of it. She would keep part ownership in the new mall. And as one condition of the sale, the mall would have to carry the Schuyler name."

Billy rubbed his ear vigorously, as if he were trying to erase Lucas's words.

"I also suggested that she should include a retail outlet for her products. She said that she wasn't in the retail business. But I told her that she could use the store for test-marketing."

"What did she say?" Henry asked.

"She said she'd think about it."

"That sounds like an offer to me," Luther said. "Who told you to make her an offer?"

126

Lucas shook his head. "It was just an idea for her to consider."

Don Appleby finally spoke: "I wonder if the Hamilton Company would settle for only part ownership."

"Billy, you should float that idea with them," Lucas suggested.

Billy said, "Okay, I will," without any enthusiasm.

"But how do we know she'd really do it?" Henry asked.

Don said, "I think it's worth a try. We have no other options."

Luther was watching Lucas closely, as if he were waiting for him to make a mistake.

"So, bang! You're right in the middle of everything," Luther snorted. "How the hell did that happen?"

Lucas shrugged.

Luther looked at each of the other committee members in turn and asked, "How the hell did that happen?"

"Nothing else was working, Luther," Henry replied.

"Why don't we write a formal proposal to show Mrs. Grant?" Don said. "Lucas can help us draft it."

Billy began to rub his forehead, faster and faster.

He said, "Ernie, draw it up like a contract. Work with Lucas on it. Do it fast. We only have a couple of weeks before Hamilton's offer expires. I'll talk to the people at Hamilton."

"Jesus!" Luther said. "Are we going to take a vote, or doesn't that matter any more?"

The "yes" vote was unanimous.

Luther was satisfied. But he was still angry.

11

The Player

On Thursday afternoon business was so slow at the garden center that Leo decided to close at five o'clock, an hour early. (Henry had left by the time Lucas arrived.)

As Leo was locking the front gate, Lucas asked, "In the mood for a cold beer? I've got a couple of six-packs waiting for me in the refrigerator."

Leo hesitated before he said, "I guess so."

"But you're not sure?"

Leo studied him for a moment.

"It's been a long, hot day. I'm sure."

Lucas knew what Leo wasn't sure about was him.

A few minutes later they were sitting on the patio outside Lucas's apartment drinking Samuel Adams beer straight from the bottle.

Lucas waited for Leo to start the conversation.

Leo seemed to be waiting, too.

Finally he said, "Things usually move at a very slow pace around here. But you've managed to shake everything up in a hurry.

How long have you been in town? A month?"

"Right."

"How do you do it?"

Lucas smiled. "Do what?"

"Whatever it is that's got everybody watching you, listening to you, trusting you."

"Maybe they're watching and listening, but nobody trusts me."

"Then why are they paying so much attention to you?"

"Because I'm from Somewhere Else. I'm not already labeled and stacked on the shelf. They don't know if my father was a failure, or my sister was an alcoholic, or my grandfather wore a dress. Leo, I grew up in a town like this. I know how it feels to walk down the street dragging your family's history behind you. I'm not carrying that baggage. It's the same with you, isn't it?"

"I'll always be an outsider anyway, for other reasons."

"Then why do you stay?"

"Because that's what I choose to do."

He's like a poker player. If you want to see his cards, you're going to pay for the privilege.

"Well, I suppose you could say that I've been adding a little excitement to the Pennington scene," Lucas said.

Leo laughed, but his eyes didn't.

"Definitely. Henry and his friends think you might be able to save their glorious shopping mall for them. Emily Grant has apparently adopted you. And you seem to have swept your landlady off her feet. Have I forgotten anyone?"

"I don't think so."

"Emily is quite a legend in this town. What is she like?"

Lucas swallowed a cold mouthful of beer. "Very strong. Very tough. And very realistic—too realistic, maybe."

"What do you mean?"

"She doesn't take emotions into account. Business isn't just about numbers. There are intangibles you've got to consider. Otherwise, you can make some serious mistakes."

"Are you one of those intangibles?"

"In this town, right now, I am."

"I'm sure they're all wondering whose side you're on."

"What do you think?"

"I don't know yet. But I'd bet that it doesn't matter to you who wins or loses. You just enjoy the game."

He thinks he knows what I'm doing. That will make it easier.

"That's true. I do enjoy it."

Leo leaned forward and said, "Be careful. Games can spin out of control."

"Is that the voice of experience?"

Lucas watched Leo try to decide how to answer.

"You could say that."

Lucas didn't respond.

Leo said, "I admire your technique."

"My technique?"

"You seem to be laid back, but you're not. You seem to be ill at ease, but you're not. You ask a lot of questions, but you don't like to answer any. And you're always watching, observing, adding things up."

"Is that what I've been doing?"

"It is. I've seen the way you handle Henry. You let him push you around for a while. You let him think he's got the upper hand. Then, all of a sudden, you're Emily Grant's best friend, and Henry is handling you with kid gloves. If I didn't give you work to do, he'd be paying you for sitting around and drinking coffee."

"You're giving me more credit than I deserve."

After a long beat, Leo said, "I don't think so. I know what

you're doing. I used to play a lot of poker."

"Really? You're famous around here for *not* playing cards or gambling."

"I haven't done either in a long time. And I never will again. But I was a player."

"You must have lost a hell of a lot."

"I won a lot, too."

"This isn't that kind of game. I'm playing with other people's money."

"And with their feelings, too. You'd better listen to your own advice—about intangibles."

Lucas raised both hands in surrender.

"You're right. I should be careful. Hey, you downed that beer in a flash. Want another one?"

"Sure."

After he had opened two more bottles, Lucas asked, "What do you do for fun, Leo?"

"Questions, and more questions."

"I think this is called making conversation."

Leo shrugged. "I'm not very sociable. I had a girlfriend for a while, in Fulton, 'til we got tired of each other. I was married for more than twenty years, but after we got divorced, I lost my interest in long-term relationships. They cost too much."

"Any kids?"

"No."

He answered that question too quickly.

"What do you do for fun, besides not going out on dates?"

Leo smiled.

"There's a double-A baseball team in Fulton. I like to go to the games. It's real small-town stuff. And there's boxing at an arena in St. Albans, south of here—it's actually a skating rink, but on a Friday night, every few weeks, they set up a ring and a couple of hundred folding chairs. Most of the fighters are local kids, but every once in a while, somebody comes through who used to be pretty good."

"Baseball. Boxing. I'd like to go with you sometime, if you don't mind."

Lucas could see that Leo was getting more comfortable. The beer was relaxing him.

"When I was in my teens," Leo said, "I lived in a small town in Upstate New York. I trained in a local gym to be a boxer. I had some talent. I could hit. But I didn't like getting hit."

"So you switched to baseball."

"No. I switched to poker."

"How do you train for that?"

"I was lucky. I met a real pro, a cardplayer who'd been at it for thirty years. Lenny Longwood was his name. He was a black dude who talked real slow and thought real fast. He was always on the road, from one town to the next, one game to the next. He always made money. I traveled with him. I packed his bags, watched his back, washed his underwear, took his clothes to the cleaners, bought the bus tickets. And he taught me how to win. And when to lose."

"Why would you lose?"

"There're a lot of reasons. You may want to give a sucker some temporary confidence. Or you may want to avoid getting your head busted. You get into all kinds of games. And you'd better have a damn good idea of who's sitting at the table with you. And whether they'll let you leave with your winnings."

"You were a professional."

"I can deal you any cards I want, and you won't know that I'm cheating."

"No way!"

"Do you have a deck of cards?"

"No."

Leo reached into the back pocket of his pants and put a box of cards on the table.

"You carry them around with you?"

"Force of habit. I haven't played in years, but I'd feel naked without them."

He opened the box, pulled out the deck, separated the jokers and handed the deck to Lucas.

"Shuffle them, cut them, do whatever you like to them."

Lucas shuffled, cut, shuffled again and handed the deck back to Leo.

Leo cut the deck once, quickly shuffled and dealt five cards to Lucas.

"What do you know? You have a full house," Leo said.

Lucas looked at his cards.

"Jacks and tens. How the hell did you do that?"

"If I want you to win, you win. If I want you to lose, you lose. But I could never pull that with another pro. That would be dangerous."

He collected the cards and put them back in the box.

"You haven't lost your touch," Lucas said.

"Neither have you. You've managed to learn a lot about me, haven't you?"

"I suppose so."

"By the way, Henry knows all about my checkered past. He's proud of the fact that he saved me from a life of sin."

"So I guess you've handled Henry, too."

They laughed and Lucas said, "But he's not the reason you stopped gambling."

"I just got tired of the life."

Leo finished his second beer and stood up.

"Thanks for the beer, Lucas. There's a fight card in St. Albans next Friday night. If you're free, it's my treat."

12

Faith

A few minutes after six that evening Lucas was sitting in the arm chair in his living room, trying to read *The New Bible Companion* but he couldn't focus on it. He found Ernie's business card in his wallet and dialed his number.

Lucas asked him if he'd drawn up the proposal for Emily.

"Yeah. It's not a formal contract, but it can be converted into one very easily."

"I'll pick it up at your office tomorrow morning. Are you going to be there around nine-thirty or ten?"

"I'll be here all morning. When do you think you'll have a chance to show it to Emily?"

"I'll call her right now."

Ernie's sullen, breathless voice became even more tentative.

"What do you think she'll do?"

Lucas didn't answer, letting the silence feed Ernie's tension.

"She won't give us an answer right away," Lucas said. "That wouldn't be any fun for her. But my guess is she'll agree to the deal."

134

"I'll see you in the morning."

Before Ernie could say anything else, Lucas hung up and pressed "six," speed-dialing Emily's number.

Cameron answered.

"Hello, Cameron. This is Lucas Murdoch. May I speak to Mrs. Grant?"

"Just a moment, please, Mr. Murdoch. I'll see if she's available."

When Emily said, "Hello, Lucas," he thought of the photograph in the library: the queen on her throne, and the orphaned princess with her enigmatic smile.

"Emily. How are you tonight?"

"Very well, as always. And you?"

"Can't complain. I've got a treat for you."

"A treat?"

"An offer from—what did you call them?—the Three Musketeers? Or was it the Servants' Children?"

Emily laughed.

"You don't speak very respectfully of your clients."

"They're not my clients. I don't care whether you take their offer or not."

"Then why are you negotiating for them?"

"Because they can't do it for themselves. They don't understand you. They never could."

"At last you're beginning to sound like the real Lucas Murdoch." After a pause, she asked, "What do you think of the offer?"

"I haven't seen the formal papers yet, but if they followed my advice, it's a perfect situation for you."

"How do you know what I'd consider perfect?"

"I may be a mystery, Emily, but you're not. You've told me how you feel."

"And if I accept the offer, what do you get out of it?"

"Nothing."

"Nonsense."

"Maybe if you invite me for lunch tomorrow, we can look over the proposal together and, as an added bonus, you can figure me out."

"Be here at noon."

"With pleasure."

He hung up before she had a chance to respond.

He walked over to the refrigerator, got a beer, sat down in the arm chair again, and drank slowly. He had almost finished it when there was a knock at the door that connected his apartment to the rest of the house. It was a soft knock. Fay.

She was wearing a long, silky robe and slippers.

"I guess Joey is off to the wars?" he said.

"He went to Boston for a few days."

"With God Knows Who, I presume. Why Boston?"

"Why indeed? I don't think they're going to the Fine Arts Museum."

"Come in."

"No, I'd rather you came upstairs."

He put his hand on her arm and pulled her gently into the apartment.

"Lucas, I'd rather not stay here."

"Memories? Your mother?"

She nodded.

"Let's go upstairs then."

In the afterglow, she was curled up against him, her naked warmth echoing his, her hand touching his chest lightly, her eyes closed.

He asked, "What was it like, all those years, taking care of your mother?"

"At first, I thought it would be a short-term kind of thing. I had come home for other reasons. And then, even after Mom got sick, I didn't think I'd have to change my plans. But it didn't turn out that way."

"What were your plans?"

She looked at Lucas, tried to decide if she would answer him.

"I just want to know you better, Fay."

She kissed his mouth softly, sighed. He stroked her hair.

"I was engaged. I thought that if Mom still needed help—a nurse, maybe, or someone to shop for her, that kind of thing—after we got married, we could hire somebody."

"But you didn't get married."

"I didn't get married."

"Who were you engaged to?"

"What's the difference who it was?"

He didn't answer.

"Why does it matter?"

Still no answer.

"Ernie Hynes. We were engaged for almost two years. I was a senior in college when he asked me to marry him."

And he's been here, all these years, married to someone else.

"He changed his mind?"

"Mom was sick and it didn't look like she'd ever get better. Ernie was just starting his law practice. He didn't have any money. He was afraid to take on that kind of burden."

"Why didn't you leave Pennington?"

"My father was dead. Joey was gone. Someone had to take care of Mom."

"Even after she died, you stayed."

"I'm not a kid any more. Where would I go?"

"And now you're taking care of Joey?"

"No. He's not my burden. Mom thought he was God's gift to her. I can't imagine why. He was always a bum. But she used to tell me, 'Faith, you've got to be more forgiving. Joey's a good boy. Just a little wild.'"

"Faith?"

"That's my name. I never liked it. I never use it. Mom was the only one who called me that. It doesn't fit a Godless girl like me."

I've seduced Faith. How appropriate.

"And you're not bitter about all this?"

"I got used to my life."

"I would have been angry. At Ernie. At Joey. At your mother."

"I was sometimes. When . . ."

She stopped herself.

"When Ernie married someone else," he said.

"Someone who had money. Well, her parents did. Not much, but a hell of a lot more than either of us had. They paid the rent on his office for a couple of years. And later, they helped him open his real estate agency."

"Love conquers all."

Her dark brown eyes studied his face for a moment, as if she were searching for sympathy, as if she were regretting everything she had told him. He softened his look, kissed her mouth, stroked her thigh.

"He isn't strong," she said. "He was afraid. He still is. He can't help it."

"And there was no one else?"

"No one who meant anything to me. Then I got tired of the

138

same routine, the same disappointment. Now, when I think about it, I'm not even sure I loved Ernie. I don't know how I could have loved him. I don't even like him."

"So you're not bitter about it?"

"Lucas, I don't want to look back. Let me enjoy you. Please."

He kissed her again and held her close.

Ernie's office was a narrow, one-story, brick building on Route Forty-Six, down the hill from the Grange. It crouched by the roadside as if it were trying not to be noticed.

"Ernest Hynes, Esq., Attorney at Law, Real Estate."

The front door opened into a walled-in reception area, where a colorless young woman sat at a gray steel desk. To her left, a large bulletin board displayed a dozen or so sheets with photos and descriptions of houses for sale or rent.

Lucas smiled at her. "I'm Lucas Murdoch. Mr. Hynes is expecting me."

The young woman returned his smile and made a call on the intercom. After a moment, she said, "Mr. Murdoch is here."

She replaced the receiver and pointed to a door behind her. "You can go right in."

Ernie was seated behind a dark wooden desk that looked much too big for him. He rose to shake Lucas's hand and motioned for him to sit down.

Getting right down to business, Ernie held out a slim packet of typewritten sheets that were clipped together.

"That's the proposal," Ernie said, in his breathless half-whisper.

Lucas didn't look at it.

"I'm having lunch with Emily at noon."

He tried to imagine Ernie as a young man, the man Fay had wanted to marry.

"You don't think she'll react to the proposal today."

"What's her hurry? She loves watching you squirm."

"As long as she agrees to do it, I don't mind squirming for a while."

Lucas nodded.

Emily is right, he thought. *Ernie and Billy are the servants' children, feeding on scraps from the table. Not worth her while. Not worth mine, either.*

"You were born in Pennington, right?"

Ernie was surprised by the question.

"Yes."

"And you've lived here all your life."

"Yes."

"Did you ever think about leaving? Maybe trying your luck somewhere else? I remember what a big step it was for me, when I decided to leave home."

"When I was young, I thought about it."

"What kept you here?"

"I wasn't comfortable anywhere else. When I passed the bar, I actually did work at a firm in New Haven. For about six months. But I could never get my bearings there. I never felt I belonged there."

"Do you think you made the right choice?"

"Sure. I can't imagine what my life would be like without Nadine—my wife—or our daughter. I know I made the right choice."

"I guess Nadine was your high school sweetheart. That's the way the story goes in small towns, isn't it?"

Lucas smiled, counterfeiting a shared, small-town-boy intimacy: "You marry your high school sweetheart. That's the way it was in my home town."

"Well, no. We didn't date until I came back from New Haven."

"Then you must have broken someone else's heart, huh?"

Ernie frowned. "Why do you say that?"

Lucas smiled blandly.

"I'm just making conversation."

Ernie seemed tense.

"Why don't you read the proposal?" he said." Make sure it's what you want."

"What she wants."

"Yeah."

"I'm not worried about that. I have confidence in you, Ernie. I'm going over to Sarge's for breakfast. I'll read it there."

Lucas stood up. Ernie followed suit and shook Lucas's hand.

"Thanks for your help," Lucas said.

On the way to the diner, Lucas changed his mind. He drove to the Cascades, and parked his car in a clearing near the entrance.

He walked through the woods slowly, treading lightly, cautiously, as if the grass were a thin sheet of ice, barely covering a deep, frigid lake.

When he reached the waterfall, he sat on a flat boulder and watched the endless, tireless flow, and listened to the quiet song of the stream.

He thought, *I won't waste my time on Ernie and Billy. Or Joey. They don't matter. They have nothing to give me.*

But he wondered if any of them mattered—Fay, Henry, Leo, Sarge, even Emily.

The watery voice of the Cascades whispered their names, over and over.

He thought, *When I'm finished with them, what difference will it make? It won't end. I'll have to search somewhere else, for*

more Fays, more Henrys. I'll have to start again. And again.

He remembered Diana's face, as pale as the snow around her, framed by her long, dark hair, her eyes staring blindly at the sky, a streak of blood across her forehead.

He remembered his wife's face, as pale as the walls of the hospital room, her eyes staring blindly at him, as if he were a stranger.

He remembered his daughter's face, pale and shadowed, her eyes turning away from him, as if he were a stranger.

He remembered the crimson, bloody spikes of the Wingthorn rose.

I could leave Pennington tonight, leave the secrets and the sins of these small-town people behind me. They would be no better off. I would be no worse.

The waterfall whispered another name: *Margot.*

Lucas shook his head, stood up and turned away.

He walked back to his car with heavier steps, as if the temperature had suddenly dropped, and the ice on the lake had become an unyielding, unbreakable barrier.

13

Wind Chimes

At lunch Emily seemed less Olympian than usual. She finished her first glass of wine quickly, and asked for a refill. She didn't pay much attention to her food.

"Something bothering you, Emily?"

She pursed her lips, considering an answer, but didn't respond.

He waited for several beats, then asked, "Would you rather be alone?"

"I'm always alone," she answered, as if she were proud of the fact.

He sipped his wine and let the silence settle between them.

She looked away from him, over his shoulder, at the window behind him. Then she looked down at the table.

She said, "Jeanette . . ."

She didn't complete the sentence.

"Jeanette's being . . . difficult."

"She's only fifteen."

"Childhood isn't an excuse. She's been a child all her life. But she hasn't behaved like this."

"What's she doing?"

"It's what she's not doing. Her tutor is on vacation for a few months—until September. But he left work for her to do over the summer. Books to read. Essays to write. Two short stories to translate from the French. I asked her how it's going. She said she's taking a couple of weeks off."

"Is that so dangerous?"

"It's not like her."

"I'm not exactly an expert on child-rearing, but . . ."

Her eyes narrowed. "I wonder if you're part of the reason."

"I doubt it. We hardly know each other."

"She doesn't meet many people. She was impressed with you."

"I don't see the connection."

"It's just a feeling I have."

Lucas smiled benignly. "I honestly don't understand what you mean."

"Perhaps I'm just looking for a fall guy," but she said the words without remorse.

"Speaking of fall guys, why don't you take a look at the mall proposal?"

"I'm not in the mood. Do you think I should do it?"

"Yes."

"I'll consider it. If I agree to do it, I'll ask my lawyers to draw up a formal contract."

"I'll pass the word to Henry and company."

"I'm not feeling sociable today, Lucas. I'd rather spend time with my flowers."

"Of course."

He shook her hand and left the house.

As he approached his car, he heard Jeanette's voice calling him. She was wearing white linen slacks and a loose-fitting, lavender blouse.

"I missed you at lunch," he said.

"How touching. We can make up for that, right now. Let's take a walk."

He followed her around the side of the house, toward the veranda.

"I'm giving you fair warning: I'm going to find out who you really are," Jeanette said.

"I've told you who I am."

She looked at him, her half-smile denying what he said.

"Have you hired a detective agency? The Pinkertons, maybe?"

"I'm doing the job myself. On the Internet."

"You'll be disappointed."

"Because of what I find out?"

"Because there's nothing to find out."

"We'll see, won't we?"

She skirted the veranda and walked toward the greenhouse.

"Are you doing this for your grandmother?"

"No. I don't intend to tell her."

"I'm sure she'd love to know."

"That's why not."

"She's worried about you."

Jeanette laughed. "I'm the last thing in the world she's worried about."

"She says you're not behaving the way you usually do."

"You mean, I'm falling behind in my homework?"

"Yes."

She smiled and said, "Oh, ye of little faith."

She stopped, pointed at the greenhouse and added, "There's her paradise. Her Garden of Eden. And she's the snake in it."

"Does she know you feel that way about her?"

"I think she'd be delighted to be called the snake in paradise. But she doesn't care how I feel about her."

She stopped near the greenhouse and said, "She's really a simple person. For her, control is everything. Whether it's her company, or me, or her beloved flowers."

"She was worried about you. She told me so."

"She's worried that I won't do what she wants me to do. That's not the same thing."

They walked toward the woods that bordered the estate.

"She cares about you."

Jeanette stopped and turned toward Lucas. She breathed deeply, looked down at the grass for a moment, then up at him. He could suddenly see past the veil of her eyes, past her mysterious half-smile.

He took a step back.

She said, "You can't remember your mother and father. All they are is a handful of photographs. And every story you hear about them tells you they were worthless failures. You have no friends. You live in the castle on the hill and wonder what it's like to live in town. What it's like to be loved."

She turned away from him and started to walk.

He followed.

They moved silently toward the woods.

She's the key, he thought.

He almost reached out to touch her, to comfort her. He shook off that feeling.

She didn't stop when she reached the edge of the woods, but entered a narrow path between the trees. It wasn't wide enough for them to walk abreast. He fell in behind her.

It was cool, shady. They passed through changing patterns of dark and light, the shimmering chiaroscuro painted by sun and leaves.

He heard soft music. Wind chimes.

He searched the branches above him. The music came closer and then he saw a glint of reflected light high above them.

"I wonder who put the wind chimes up in that tree," he said.

"I did," she replied.

"Why?"

She stopped, turned, and leaned against the trunk of a tree. "That was my subversive little plot. I always loved to climb. When I was younger, twelve, thirteen, I used to climb this tree. And I hung the chimes in it as high as I could. I would sit up there on a branch and close my eyes and listen to the wind making music, and pretend that my mother and father were waiting for me at home, and that I had an older brother and a kid sister."

"I've seen a set of chimes like those in the Cascades."

"They're mine, too. And there are others."

"Do you still climb up there and listen to the music?"

"Not any more."

Lucas didn't know why she had trusted him enough to tell him who she really was. Then she lowered the veil. She was, again, the icy, distant, orphan princess.

Lucas tried to think of her that way, but he couldn't. He wondered if she had changed the rules of the game too much for him to keep playing it.

"You can run, Mr. Murdoch, but you can't hide. I'll find you," she said.

"I suppose you will."

He left her there, in the shadows, listening to the quiet music of her wind chimes.

That evening, Lucas called Margot.

"I thought about calling you a couple of days ago . . ." she began, excitedly.

"But you don't have my phone number."

"I guess it's Top Secret—Eyes Only?"

"If it were to fall into the wrong hands, who knows what might happen to the Free World?"

"I wanted to tell you that I got a job. I start on Monday."

"That's great."

"It's with a company called Shelby Associates. They're management consultants headquartered in Boston, but they just opened a satellite office in St. Albans. Why St. Albans, you ask?"

"Because office space there is cheap, and consultants spend half their time on the road anyway, meeting with clients. And the rest of the time, they can do their work anywhere."

"Have you heard of Shelby?"

"They've been around for a while."

"You sound different, Luke."

"I'm a week older. Age must be catching up with me."

He could picture her shaking her head.

"You must be tired," she said. "There's no edge in your voice. Or are the walls finally coming down?"

"I'd like to see you tonight."

"I'd love to see you. The last time we were together, it was like we weren't together."

"Would you mind if I bring my toothbrush?"

"Well, I may be married and I may be short, but I definitely have enough toothpaste for both of us."

"I'll be there in a little while."

On the drive to Fulton, he thought of a little girl, closing her eyes, shutting out the world, listening to the wind's music and dreaming that she was someone else. And then he thought of his daughter.

Did she dream Jeanette's dreams: her mother and father loving each other, and loving her?

He decided that he would ask her. Soon.

As Lucas approached the door, he thought, *I shouldn't be here. This is the wrong time to see her.*

He rang the bell and, a moment later, she took his hand and led him inside.

"Have you eaten?"

He nodded.

"Would you like some wine?"

He shook his head.

He leaned down and kissed her mouth. He put his arms around her slim, strong body and kissed her again, open-mouthed.

He pulled away and said, "I'm not making you any promises."

"I don't care."

He searched the dark, blue shadows of her eyes, as if he were looking for a place to hide.

"I won't tell you that I love you," he said.

"Don't worry about me. I can take care of myself."

He stroked her hair, kissed her forehead.

"Can you?"

"Yes."

She took his hand and led him up to her bedroom.

He wondered again if it would be different with her, or

would he simply repeat the same tired dance steps.

It was different, as if he were both of them, feeling her kisses and caresses, and those that he gave her, too. As if they were reflections of each other, sharing every sensation, every pleasure.

He had never felt that way, not even with Diana. Not even with his wife, when they were young.

And when the pleasure had ebbed and was becoming a memory, he held Margot in his arms, in the darkness, and tried not to remember the wasteland behind Jeanette's smile.

Maybe Pennington doesn't matter. Maybe I don't need to be there. I have to see Beth.

14

Beth

At ten o'clock on Sunday night, Lucas waited near the entrance to a thirty-story office building on the upper West Side of Manhattan. A pleasant Hudson River breeze ruffled the clouds and cooled the streets. Lucas was wearing gray slacks and a blue blazer.

Spector had told him that Beth was working at the radio station on Sunday and that her shift would end at ten p.m.

He tried to imagine what he would say to her, but couldn't. He wanted to sit somewhere with her, in a quiet place, and help her understand what he had done, and why he had done it. But he couldn't seem to find the words.

About twenty minutes after ten, she came out of the building alone and walked toward Lucas. She was a tall, slender, attractive woman in her late twenties. Her face was a softer version of Lucas's face, but when she saw him, the line of her mouth hardened and her gray eyes froze.

"Daddy dear, what a surprise. What brings you to town? On the trail of a new girlfriend? Or does a failing company need your tender mercies? How about firing everyone whose pension isn't vested yet?"

"I'm not working any more. You know that, Beth."

"I still don't know why."

"I hear you're doing very well. That you've been promoted. That they're mentioning your name on the air now."

"You hear? I'm not famous enough for the gossip columns, so you must have hired somebody to spy on me."

"They're just keeping me up to date about you."

He pointed to a coffee shop across the street. "Would you like to sit down for a few minutes, have a cup of coffee, and talk?"

"No, thanks. I'm tired. I want to go home and get a good night's sleep."

"Please, Beth."

"Please? That's a new word for you, isn't it? You say it almost as if you know what it means."

"Could you give me a few minutes?"

She started toward the corner. "My apartment is a fifteen-minute walk from here. You can walk with me, if you like. That's the best I can do for you."

"Okay."

"I haven't seen you in quite a while—more than a year, isn't it? And you're still not back at work?"

"That's right."

"I realize you have enough money to last forever. And keep me in the chips. And, of course, pay the bills at Grassmere."

She stopped, tilted her head to one side and said, "Oh, speaking of Grassmere, have you been there lately?"

"I keep informed about her."

"Her? You mean Katharine Murdoch? Your wife? My mother? Or is there some other wacko broad you've got stashed there?"

Lucas looked into her eyes and saw Jeanette's eyes looking back at him.

"Beth, I just want to talk."

"I'll give Mom your best, when I see her. Hopefully, this week, she'll know that I'm her daughter."

"I wish we could . . ."

"She's probably forgotten you by now. I hope she has."

"Beth . . ."

"Don't worry, Daddy. I don't hate you. You don't matter enough to me. That's the way it's been for a long time. We never did anything together, did we? You were too busy wowing Wall Street—and any woman you could get your hands on."

"I know what I was."

"And what are you now? Still on the run? Still hiding from your wife and your daughter?"

Lucas thought about explaining what he was doing, but the words eluded him.

"Mom is a good person, but she's not nearly as strong as I am. She couldn't keep herself together. She needed you, and I wasn't able to help her. I still can't."

She stopped and turned to him.

"When I was little, there were so many times I wished you were with me. I wanted you to tuck me in and kiss me goodnight. Or help me with my homework. Or read me a story. Or tell me . . . But I got over that. I don't need you any more, Daddy."

She started to walk away, then turned. "And I never will."

15

The Hunter

As they walked to the Cascades on Monday morning, Fay was quiet, reserved. Lucas pretended not to notice, but he knew she was wondering where he had been all weekend, a weekend that she had expected to spend with him.

When they ran together, she pushed herself hard. He let her pull ahead briefly, then accelerated past her and left her, gasping for breath, halfway up a steep hill. He ran back and sat down beside her in the grass.

He felt calm and focused. It was only a matter of time now.

When she had caught her breath, she asked, "Where were you this weekend?"

She searched his face intently, as if the explanation were written there. But his face told her nothing.

"I had things to do."

He had been with Margot on Friday night, all day Saturday, and Saturday night, too. Late Sunday morning, he had come back from Fulton to Pennington, showered and changed his clothes, and driven to Manhattan.

 154

"I missed you," Fay said.

He reached out and stroked her hair.

"I missed you, too, Faith."

She frowned.

"Don't call me that."

"It's your name, isn't it?"

"I don't like it. You know I don't like it."

He kissed her forehead. "Relax. I'm just playing with you."

She shook her head.

"It's not a game."

"Because your mother called you Faith?"

He kissed her mouth, keeping her off balance.

"Please, Lucas."

He changed direction. "If you're worried about where I was this weekend, I can tell you that I wasn't with another woman. I'm a one-woman man—Fay."

"It wasn't another woman?"

"No."

He kissed her mouth again, lightly, and said, "But I can tell you, from my own experience: You can't take off your past and hang it in the closet."

"Why is my past so important to you?"

"Because I'm beginning to care about you. I want to know you better."

Lucas could see she was confused, uncomfortable with his probing, but flattered that he had told her—for the first time—that he cared about her.

"Leaving me alone all weekend isn't the best way to show me you care. Neither is calling me Faith."

Lucas kissed her cheek.

"But your name is part of the truth about you."

"You haven't told me very much about yourself. Don't I deserve the truth, too?"

"This weekend, I went to New York to help a friend of mine. Someone I used to work with. I haven't seen him for a while. He's having a hard time. He sounded like he was going over the edge. So I went to help him get back on track."

"Is he all right now?"

"I think so."

Fay took his hand and held it in both of hers.

"You have to understand," she said. "It's been a long time since I've let something like this happen to me. I'm not used to it. I feel vulnerable, and I don't like that feeling. You're not going to hurt me, are you?"

"Why would I hurt you?"

"There are times when I think you want to."

"You should know there are no guarantees."

She let go of his hand, and of the subject.

She said, "Joey's having breakfast with us this morning."

"You mean he's actually awake at this ungodly hour?"

"I guess he struck out last night."

She smiled, but her eyes kept watching Lucas cautiously, uneasily, as if she expected him to say something unpleasant. Again.

At breakfast, Joey looked his age. He was wearing a shabby blue silk bathrobe, his hair was uncombed, and there were heavy, dark circles under his eyes. He was not in a good mood.

"Christ, I had better weekends when I was at sea."

"Are you still going out with the girl I met in Fulton that night?" Lucas asked.

"Jill? No. She started getting that old familiar look in her

156

eye, like she wanted to lock me up and throw away the key. I've seen it before. Too many times. I don't need that marriage crap any more."

"You're such a prize," Fay said.

He poured himself a second cup of coffee, looked at Fay for a moment, and asked, "Hey, Lucas. What about Jill's friend? You still seeing her?"

Lucas shook his head.

"No. I was just doing you a favor, remember?"

Joey wouldn't drop the subject.

"But the two of you waltzed out of that club like you were headed straight for the sack."

"We had a cup of coffee. We talked for an hour or so. We had nothing in common."

"She quit her job. Did you know that?"

"How would I?"

Joey looked at Fay and said, "Jill thought the two of you hit it off."

"We didn't."

"So now it's you and Fay, huh?"

Fay groaned. "Why don't you just eat your breakfast and spare us your wisdom?"

Joey smiled.

"Hey, don't get me wrong, Fay. I'm glad you've finally got something going. Christ, it's about time."

He smiled again.

Fay pointed her fork at him, as if it were a loaded gun.

"Thanks for your concern. Lucas, do you want more eggs? More toast?"

"No, thanks. Joey, I hear you were your mother's favorite. Is that true?"

"Yeah. Yeah. It's true."

Lucas asked Fay, "Why do you think she felt that way?"

She shook her head, as if she didn't understand the question.

"Lucas . . ."

"You took care of your mother, didn't you? You spent half your life doing that, while your brother was gone. Why weren't *you* her favorite? It doesn't make sense."

Fay covered her eyes with her hands for a moment. "I don't know. Does it matter?"

"I think mothers always love their sons more," Joey said. "That's just the way it is."

"Maybe so," Lucas agreed.

"Yeah, it's human nature."

"Mom never said 'thank you' to me," Fay said. "No matter what I did. Human nature, huh?"

"And did that make you angry?" Lucas asked.

"Sure, it did."

"Did you ever tell her how you felt?"

"I tried a few times. She would look like she was listening to me, but then she would just turn away, without reacting to what I said, as if she were deaf. Which she wasn't."

"Did you ever tell anyone else?"

She looked at her watch. "I've got to get to work."

She stood up.

"Will I see you tonight?" she asked Lucas.

"Yes."

She leaned forward, kissed his mouth and left.

Joey shook his head. "I can't figure out why you're interested in her."

"She's very special to me," Lucas said, and he meant it.

When Lucas arrived at work that afternoon, Henry almost ran to meet him.

"Did you hear from Emily yet?"

"No."

"How did she react to the proposal?"

"She didn't. She had other things on her mind."

"Did you tell her you thought she should do it?"

"Yes. But you know what that's worth."

"Did she read the proposal while you were there?"

"No."

"Did she say she would?"

"She said she'd show it to her lawyers. They'll draw up a contract, if they decide it's worth her while."

Henry's eyes narrowed.

He said, "God only knows what they'll come up with."

"Speaking of God, when is your next Bible class?"

Henry looked at Lucas blankly, for a moment. Then he managed to refocus his attention.

"Tomorrow evening, at my place. You know where that is?"

"I think it's just down the street from Fay's house."

"Right. The address is two thirty-five."

"What time should I be there?"

"Seven."

"I have to warn you that I've never been a churchgoer. I'm probably a lost cause."

Henry smiled sourly. "From what I've seen, you're a quick study."

"What's on my schedule today?"

"You could help Leo at the counter."

"No, no. Give me some real work."

Henry started to disagree, but then nodded. "We just got

in a shipment of patio furniture. There are three different styles of tables and chairs. Put one set of each on display—on the lawn out front. You'll have to assemble them. And store the rest in the stock room, in the space behind the shelves. Billy will help you. Take your time."

Billy Miles, Jr., was at the counter with Leo.

Billy was in his early twenties. He was tall, slim and angular, with an expression that combined aggressiveness and hostility in equal measures. There was nothing tentative about him.

Hardly the image of his father, Lucas thought.

Lucas said, "He actually came in on time?"

"Who says there are no miracles any more?"

Lucas smiled. "Maybe I'll start going to church again."

He left Henry and walked over to the counter.

"Hi, Leo. Billy."

"Henry's been pacing around all morning," Leo said. "He couldn't wait for you to come in. He was going to call you, but he doesn't have your phone number."

"My phone is for outgoing calls only."

"So, what's the scoop on the shopping center?"

"Emily's in no hurry. She's sitting at the poker table with a royal flush. And she can go 'all in' any time she wants to."

Billy asked, "What's the old lady like? I know my dad hates her guts."

"She's tough. She doesn't trust anyone. She's used to getting her way. Always has. Probably always will."

"Probably?" Leo asked.

"One never knows."

"How'd you get so chummy with her?" Billy asked.

"I'm the new game in town. It won't last."

Leo asked, "We still on for the fights in St. Albans on Friday?"

"Yes."

Lucas turned to Billy: "Did Henry tell you what's on our agenda this afternoon?"

Billy smiled slyly. "Yeah. And I think it should take all afternoon, don't you?"

Leo laughed.

"Sure."

The cartons containing the patio furniture were piled up on wooden skids behind the center. Lucas selected three that he set aside for assembly. Then he and Billy began to move the other cartons from the skids to the stock room. Billy insisted on several minutes of rest after each carton was transferred.

When there were only three boxes left on the first skid, Billy sat down on one, took a pack of cigarettes from his pocket and offered it to Lucas.

"No, thanks. I quit a long time ago."

"Afraid of getting cancer?"

"I was into long-distance running. So I gave up smoking."

"Win any races?"

"A few."

"Ten-K's? Marathons?"

"Both."

Billy lit a cigarette and inhaled.

He said, "I did some running in high school. Gave it up in college."

"Why?"

Billy smiled in a self-conscious, but convincing attempt to look wicked.

"Girls. Booze. Sex."

"Did you make the varsity?"

Billy laughed. "I made everything I could get my hands on."

"What was your major?"

"Business."

"When did you graduate?"

"I dropped out in my junior year."

"How did your father feel about that?"

"He was pissed, but what could he do? I'm no student."

"He must have been disappointed."

"I guess."

"Have you been working here since then?"

"No. I drove a truck for a delivery company for a couple of years. Got tired of that. Worked at Willoughby's for a while. That's the mail-order company down on Forty-Six. Ernie's wife owns it."

Billy smiled. "They call it a fulfillment center. You bet it was. Ernie's daughter Lisa works there. We had a little fulfillment together, you know what I mean?"

"They fired you."

"Yeah. So I got a job here."

"What about the future? This is a dead end, isn't it?"

Billy took a deep drag on his cigarette and exhaled most of the smoke through his nostrils.

"I'm young. I've got time."

"Don't waste it."

At about eight that night, Fay knocked on Lucas's door. When he opened it, she moved back a few steps.

Lucas smiled. "Afraid to come in?"

"Joey's home. I don't think we can . . ."

Her eyes caressed his face, his shoulders, his chest.

Lucas knew that every time he touched her, another barrier between them was shattered. Every time he touched her, she needed him more. But today, he had begun to undermine her confidence in him. Today, he had begun to build new barriers. She wasn't sure how to feel about him.

"We can. Here."

She shook her head.

"Your mother doesn't live here any more."

She looked past him, into the bare, shabby room. He could almost see memories reflected in her eyes.

"I can't."

He took her hand, firmly.

"Come in. Talk to me. That's all."

She leaned forward, pressed herself against him, hiding her face in his chest.

"Lucas," she whispered.

He put his arm around her waist and pulled her closer.

She leaned back and he kissed her mouth, her neck, her mouth again. She felt the hard muscles of his arms and shoulders.

"Come in," he said.

He closed the door behind them and led her to the bedroom.

He switched on the lamp next to his bed, but she switched it off and undressed quickly, as if she were afraid of being caught. He slipped out of his clothes slowly, making her wait.

He made her wait for her orgasms, too. He caressed her slowly, patiently, drawing out the pleasure, building it touch by touch, kiss by kiss, stroke by stroke, until the ripples started, peaked, started again.

And when she was resting in his arms, breathing deeply, wearily, he whispered, "My Faith."

She pretended not to hear him.

He whispered her name again.

"Lucas, please."

"What's the matter?"

"Don't spoil it."

"Don't you see? It doesn't matter where we make love. Or what I call you."

"It does to me."

"No, no. This is your mother's bedroom. This is where all those years went by. All those years when she didn't say, 'thank you.' And still, I can give you pleasure here. Can't I, Faith?"

She pulled away and sat up in the bed.

"I don't know why you're doing this."

"Doing what?"

"Why do you keep talking about my mother? She's gone. I don't have to be Faith any more."

"But you are Faith. You can't pretend not to be. You weren't born on the day she died."

"Why does that matter to you?"

"I want you to tell the truth."

"Leave me alone!"

She began to search through her pile of clothing, found her panties and slipped into them, found her bra and put it on.

Lucas sat up in bed, but didn't try to stop her.

She dressed quickly, then stood by the bed and looked at him.

"I thought you cared for me," she said. "That's what you told me. I don't understand."

"I'm older than you. I've learned that you have to be honest about who you are. What you did. Why you did it. It isn't easy. But I've done it."

"I still don't understand."

"I want you to tell me what it really felt like, all those years. Living here with your mother. Cooking for her. Cleaning up after her. Watching Ernie Hynes get married to someone else because of

her. Never hearing 'thank you, Faith, thank you.'"

"Damn it!"

She left him in the dark, left the apartment and slammed the door shut.

Lucas sat on the bed, savoring the moment.

A few minutes later, he got dressed, took a beer from the refrigerator, opened it and drank several swallows.

He sat down on the couch and nodded, as if he had just reminded himself of something he had forgotten to do. He picked up his cell phone from the end table and punched a quick-dial button.

When Margot answered, he said, "Hi. It's Luke."

Her voice was warm and confident: "How are you, dear?"

"Fine."

"I wanted to call you last night but, of course, I don't have your phone number. Why don't I have it?"

"I told you: I don't know how long I'll be here."

"Be where? All I know is that you're in Pennington. And I'm not. Luke, after this weekend, don't I belong in your life?"

"I won't be able to see you for a while."

"What's wrong? Did I disappoint you?"

"No."

"Are you angry about something I said?"

"No."

"I'm in love with you. And I don't know where you live. I don't even have your phone number. Isn't that ridiculous? I have to just wait for you to appear at my door."

"I need time."

"For what?"

"Margot . . ."

"Will I ever see you again?"

"I don't know."

"When we're together, everything feels right for me. Doesn't it feel that way for you?"

He didn't answer.

"Let me share your life, Luke. I'm not afraid."

"It's a bad idea. You'll get hurt."

"You're hurting me more, by not letting me love you."

"You'll regret it."

"Come see me tonight."

"I can't."

There was a long, empty pause.

She said, "If you change your mind, I'll be here."

He pressed the "end" button.

He wondered if he would ever see Margot again.

On Tuesday morning, Lucas walked to the Cascades by himself. He knew Fay wouldn't be with him. She was angry and confused. He would leave her alone for another day or two.

It was warm and damp. He ran almost the whole way to the waterfall and back, as fast as he could, up and down hill, drinking the heavy, wet air, pushing himself to the limit, until the forest was just a blur of greens and browns and shadows.

He ate breakfast at Sarge's Diner. Ernie was there, with Luther Avedon. Lucas sat at their table.

"No word yet?" Ernie asked.

"No word."

Luther was attacking a stack of pancakes as if they were on the Ten-Most-Wanted list.

He snarled, "Damn bitch."

"She may never get back to us," Ernie said.

Luther repeated, "Damn bitch."

166

"We'll hear from her," Lucas said.

Ernie sulked. "Henry says she didn't even read the proposal."

"We've done all we can do. Now it's up to her."

Luther chewed his food fiercely. Lucas ate quickly, made some empty comments, and left.

He spent the next few hours in his car, slowly driving east on Route Forty-Six with no destination in mind, through Fulton, all the way to St. Albans—about forty-five miles—and back to Fay's house. Both Fay and Joey were at work.

Lucas thumbed through *The New Bible Companion*, but couldn't concentrate on what he was reading. He went outside and sat at the table on the patio.

He watched a pair of crows circle each other in the sky, dipping and soaring, spreading their wings to ride on updrafts, swooping down to perch together on the branch of a tree. One of the birds began to sing a raucous crow song, and Lucas remembered sitting with Margot by the lake, listening to that song, listening to her translate it for him.

He closed his eyes for a moment. He was ready to think about Henry's Bible study class, and to plan for it.

16

Revelation

At Henry's house that evening, Don Appleby answered the door.

"Come in," Don said, shaking Lucas's hand. "Nice to see you."

Don was wearing a dark blue suit, a white shirt, a navy blue tie and a serious, sympathetic expression, like the greeter at a funeral parlor.

He pointed the way to the living room. "Go right in."

The house was sparsely furnished. Furniture in the living room had been moved to one side to leave an open space for a podium near the fireplace and several rows of folding chairs. There was a slim, red-covered book on the seat of each chair.

About twenty people were standing in small groups, speaking softly, almost fearfully, as if they knew they were in the church of a vengeful, rather than a loving, God.

Billy was there, with Sarge and his wife, Luther, Ernie, and a woman Lucas had never seen before.

Billy invited Lucas to join them.

"This is a surprise," Ernie said. "Was Henry expecting you?"

"Yes."

"Lucas, this is my wife, Nadine."

She was a pale, slender woman, whose eyes kept moving nervously from side to side, as if searching for something she had lost. Arthritis had begun to deform her fingers, and the tight line of her mouth reflected constant pain.

She extended her hand.

Lucas took it gently in his. "Glad to meet you, Nadine."

"You're in for quite an experience," she said. "Henry is wonderful. Wonderful."

"So I've heard."

"He doesn't just know the Bible: he has a passion for it."

"Sounds like he missed his calling."

"He was at the Seminary in Hartford, wasn't he?" Sarge said. To Lucas, he added, "That was a long time before I came back to Pennington."

"He was there for almost two years," Billy said, "but he told us he didn't feel worthy of the ministry."

Nadine placed one hand over her heart.

"He's doing God's work," she said, "and he's doing it better than Reverend Stokes, if you ask me. This is my church."

Lucas asked Billy, "Your wife isn't here tonight?"

"Helen's never been to one of Henry's classes. She doesn't go to church, either. She's not a believer. She was when she was young. Maybe someday, I'll be able to bring her back."

Ernie whispered, "I guess you've heard nothing from Emily."

"Nothing."

A moment later, Henry came in and walked directly to the podium without greeting anyone. All conversations died instantly.

Everyone watched Henry, silently, expectantly.

He was wearing a dark grey suit, a white shirt and a black string tie. His red hair shone brightly, like a flame on a dark candle. He opened the Bible on the podium and, without looking up, gestured toward the folding chairs.

Lucas sat in the back row, next to Sarge and Ellie, who seemed, as always, distant and distracted. The red-covered book on each seat was a copy of *The New Testament*.

Henry scanned the pages of the open Bible for a minute or two. Don Appleby tip-toed into the room and sat in the first row. Silence hung in the air like an unspoken threat.

Finally, Henry looked up and said without warmth, "Good evening. Welcome," as he scrutinized each face in the audience, one by one.

Several people murmured "Good evening" under their breaths.

"Good evening, Henry," Nadine said, in a loud, clear voice.

Henry smiled at her. "Good evening, Nadine."

He kept scanning their faces, nodding his head slightly in recognition of each person. When he saw Lucas, he smiled again.

"Tonight," Henry said, "we shall read from *The Revelation of Saint John the Divine*. Page one hundred and eighty. These are the words, the visions, and the dreams of a great prophet. He takes us with him on a journey to the end of days—the end of time."

He paused dramatically.

"You may ask, 'Who was the author of this book?' We think we know: we think he was the disciple John, 'whom Jesus loved'. John, the brother of James. Jesus called these brothers, His disciples, the 'sons of thunder.'"

Henry looked around at his audience.

"We believe it was Saint John, 'whom Jesus loved'—the same

Saint John who wrote one of the Gospels, and three Epistles—who wrote this *Book of Revelation*."

He leaned forward over the podium and asked, "The word Gospel comes from the Old English word Godspell. What does Godspell mean?"

Nadine burst out, "'Good news!' The good news of our Savior's coming to Earth!"

Henry shouted, "Amen!" and the rest echoed him.

Henry repeated "Amen" softly.

He said, "*Revelation* is what we call an apocalyptic vision. It speaks of dreadful things—earthquakes and demons and monsters. But it tells us not to fear the end of days—because in the war between God and the Devil, in that eternal war, God will be victorious. He will triumph. He will surely triumph!"

"Amen!" Nadine said, too loudly.

"And although we must suffer, because we are sinners— because we are *sinners*—we will be saved. For He came to save us. He became flesh like us, He became human, to share our suffering— even to die for us. And when He returns, if we repent our sins, He will free us all, forever."

Nadine: "Amen!"

The others echoed, "Amen!"

Then Henry led the way through *Revelation*, selecting a few verses, skipping many of them, reciting the words softly, sometimes almost chanting them, sometimes explaining them, but always keeping his audience tightly focused on him, his soft voice, his eyes, his presence.

"The first words of this Book—the very first words—should comfort us, for they tell us that this is 'The Revelation of Jesus Christ, which God gave unto Him, to shew unto His servants things which must shortly come to pass; and He sent and signified it by His angel unto his servant John . . .' This is a message sent to John by God, by

Jesus. Then let us rejoice, even at the start—let us have no fear, for we shall see the end of days through the eyes of God Himself."

"Amen!"

Henry paused for a moment and, leaning forward, searched the faces before him.

"Perhaps that word *shortly* puzzles you. For this Book is almost two thousand years old. And the end of days did not come shortly after this Revelation to Saint John. But the meaning is clear: in God's vast Eternity—vast beyond our imagining—what is a year, or a century, or a millennium, or a *thousand* millenniums? A drop in His ocean of time. No more than that. Our lifetimes come and go in the snap of a finger. But He is forever."

Henry smiled and read, "'I am Alpha and Omega, the beginning and the ending, saith the Lord, which is, and which was, and which is to come, the Almighty.'"

Henry fed their fears: "'And I looked, and behold a pale horse: and his name that sat on him was Death, and Hell followed with him. And Power was given unto them over the fourth part of the earth, to kill with the sword, and with hunger, and with death, and with the beasts of the earth.'"

He comforted them: "'And I saw heaven opened, and behold a white horse; and he that sat upon him was called Faithful and True, and in righteousness he doth judge and make war.'"

With anger, he banished Satan: "'And the devil that deceived them was cast into the lake of fire and brimstone, where the beast and the false prophet are, and shall be tormented day and night, for ever and ever.'"

He promised them Paradise: "'And he carried me away in the spirit to a great and high mountain, and shewed me that great city, the holy Jerusalem, descending out of heaven from God.'"

And he warned them: "We can join Him in that New Jerusalem—we *will* join Him there ("Amen!")—but only if we wash

ourselves clean of our sins." ("Amen! Amen!")

Henry spoke for more than an hour, shaping the words with his hands, his eyes, the movements of his body. By the time he bowed his head in silent prayer and said his last "Amen," he was exhausted.

"Amen!" Nadine said, too loudly.

"Amen," the rest of the audience said, softly.

This isn't a class, Lucas thought, *it's a revival meeting.*

He was more certain than ever that he was on the right track, and that now was the time to begin.

Henry remained at the podium, his head bowed, his hands folded on the open Bible, as everyone filed past him, thanking him, praising him. Lucas waited until only he and Don remained.

"I'd like to speak to Henry privately," Lucas said.

Don shook hands with Henry and left.

Lucas stood across the podium from Henry silently.

After a minute or two, Henry looked up and asked, "Is there something you wanted to tell me?"

"I need your advice."

Henry walked around the podium and sat down, wearily, on one of the folding chairs.

He said, "I'm very tired."

He wiped a bead of sweat from his forehead.

"I won't keep you long. But you're the only one I can ask about this."

Henry's dark eyes were suddenly suspicious.

"I'm listening."

Lucas sat down next to him. "It's about a dream I had. Last night. I almost never dream any more. If I do, I can't remember what I've dreamed. This was different. I can still see it clearly."

Lucas paused, looked down at the floor for a moment, as if it were difficult for him to continue.

"Go on."

"In the dream, I'm walking in the streets of a city. It's late at night. It's very dark. The streets are completely empty. No people. No traffic. The lights are off in the store windows and the office buildings. And there don't seem to be any street lamps, either. There's just the light of the moon. A full moon. And the stars."

Henry leaned forward wearily. Lucas paused again, then continued.

"I don't know where I'm going, but I'm afraid to stop. And then I see a church ahead of me. It's very small, crowded in between two big office buildings. It has a tiny steeple, with a cross at the top. A black cross."

Henry's eyes narrowed. He leaned back, folding his arms over his chest.

"The church doors are wide open. The light from inside shines out into the street. I run toward the church. It's completely empty. Except for a man standing at the altar. He's dressed in a dark suit. He's tall, slim. He has red hair."

Henry's arms tightened against his chest.

"He's gesturing wildly with his hands, reaching up to the sky. He seems to be preaching—to a congregation that isn't there. I'm in the shadows at the back of the church. He doesn't notice me. He says, 'Hear me, hear me, brothers and sisters. Sinners, hear me. I speak the truth. Hear me. There is sin, but no salvation. There is sin, but no forgiveness. There is sin, but there is no Savior.'"

Henry stood up suddenly, walked to the podium and stood behind it. He rested his hands on the Bible. Lucas followed and stood facing him, with the Bible between them.

"He says, 'There is no goodness. For there is no God. Only the Devil. No Heaven. Only Hell. And we will all be there together someday, you and I. Forever.' And then he comes down from the altar. He walks up the aisle to where I'm standing. I try to hide in

the shadows, but he sees me. He reaches out and touches me with his hand and says, 'Welcome to Hell, brother!' That's when I woke up."

"What do you want me to do?" Henry whispered.

"I'm not sure. You seem to understand things like this."

Henry shook his head.

"I understand the word of God. As it is given to us. I can't tell you what your dream means."

"It was so clear. As if it were really happening. I can still see the church. The minister."

Henry raised his right hand, as if he were about to swear an oath, and said, "A minister would not deny God." He sighed. "Lucas. I'm tired. I can't help you."

"Thanks for listening. I'll see you tomorrow."

Henry nodded.

Henry wasn't at work on Wednesday.

Leo said, "He called me at home late last night and told me he was taking a couple of days off."

"I'm not surprised. He looked exhausted after his Bible class."

"You really went to one of those Holy Roller meetings?"

"Yes."

"That's hard to believe."

"Have you ever been?"

"No. I keep away from religion."

"Why?"

Leo laughed. "Can you imagine how boring it would be to spend eternity in Heaven? All the card players would be in Hell."

"I thought you don't play cards any more."

"That doesn't mean I can't reminisce."

Leo moved a little closer and asked, "What was it like? What was he like?"

Lucas thought for a moment. "It isn't a class, and he isn't a teacher. He's a preacher. And he's pretty good at it. He puts on quite a show."

"Did he convert you?"

Lucas smiled and shook his head.

"Not yet, anyway."

On Wednesday evening, Lucas called Emily.

He asked if she and her lawyers had reached a decision about the shopping mall.

"No. I'll let you know. Cameron has your phone number, doesn't he?"

"No. During the week, I'm at the garden center every afternoon. And Saturday mornings until noon. You can call me there."

"You don't have a phone?"

"I have one."

"Doesn't it accept incoming calls?"

"Not many. There are exceptions, of course."

"But I'm not one of them."

He waited a beat before he asked, "How's Jeanette?"

"I'm not sure. She's doing her work, but she's so hard to read. She enjoys being mysterious." Her voice had an edge to it when she added, "She reminds me of you, Lucas."

"It's one way to keep you interested in us."

"If I were you, I wouldn't count on that."

"I've been warned."

She hung up without saying "goodbye."

On Thursday morning, Fay surprised Lucas: she decided to go to the Cascades with him.

They walked together silently, but she seemed very calm, without a trace of anger. When they ran together, she didn't push herself too hard. And when they sat on the grass, resting, she watched the clouds for a while, as if he weren't even there.

He didn't break the silence.

"I still don't understand why you've said the things you have," she finally said, in a voice that sounded different.

"I just . . ."

She interrupted him: "I don't care. It doesn't matter to me why you did it. I'm grateful to you. I know you weren't trying to help me. But I'm grateful, anyway."

"For what?"

"You've made me look at myself, forced me to be more honest about myself."

"About your feelings?"

"Yes. And even about my name."

She leaned forward, resting her elbows on her drawn-up knees.

"I'm Faith Geneen. That's who I've always been. That's who I'll always be."

"And who is Faith?"

"Why do you want to know? It isn't because you care about me."

"I *do* care about you."

"I'm not very sophisticated, Lucas. Small-town girl and all that. But I'm not a fool."

He didn't respond.

She said, "I'm going away for a few days."

"Where?"

"To Providence."

"Faith goes to Providence. Sounds kind of religious, doesn't it?"

"Yes. Very Puritan. Like one of those depressing Nathaniel Hawthorne stories."

"Why are you going there?"

"I think *I'll* be the mysterious one for a change."

"Not even a clue?"

"Not a hint."

She closed her eyes for a moment, then opened them and looked at him as if she had expected him to disappear.

She said, "It's been a long time since I've had a sexual relationship, and I got too caught up in the pleasure of it. I even began to get romantic about you."

She studied his face for a moment.

"But there's no romance in you, is there, Lucas? I wonder if you could love someone."

"Not someone like Ernie Hynes."

She smiled.

"You could, if you were me back then, when Ernie was still handsome and charming. When he still thought he was going to do important things some day. When we walked together here, in the Cascades, holding hands, and sat by the waterfall, imagining what our future would be like."

"But you weren't part of his future."

"He couldn't help it. He had no money. He was afraid my mother would be too big a burden for him. And he wasn't brave enough to take a chance."

"Not much of a hero."

"That's true, I suppose. But what did Faith do? Did she tell Ernie that she loved him and wanted to marry him, no matter what? That she'd talk to her brother and work out a way for both of them to support Mom and still live their own lives? Did she even try? She didn't. Where was my courage?"

"Why didn't you work something out?"

"I don't know. I guess it was easier to hate my mother instead. And Ernie and Nadine. And Joey, of course."

"Do you still hate them?"

"No. That was an easy habit to kick. And you know, when I think back, I have some doubts about how I felt then. Maybe I was afraid to get married. Maybe I wasn't sure I loved Ernie. It was so long ago I really don't remember."

"And now, how do you feel?"

"I'm breaking the habit, cold turkey."

"Just like that?"

She nodded. "It really was over a long time ago. But I had settled into a comfortable groove. I would be all the things Joey wasn't: responsible, moral, self-sacrificing, bitter. But that was nonsense."

She stood up and stretched.

"I'll be back on Sunday. But I don't think that matters any more to you, or to me either."

He sat and watched her walk away.

Fay was rewriting his script. Because of him, she might actually be better, stronger.

He shrugged.

You win some, you lose some.

When Lucas arrived at work on Friday, Henry was showing

Billy Miles, Jr., how to set up a display of decorative vases. Billy was bored and restless, as usual, but Henry kept repeating himself, patiently, making sure the boy understood exactly what he had to do.

Lucas watched them closely for a few minutes. Then he smiled.

There is no God, no forgiveness. There is no Heaven, only Hell.

Leo waved to him from behind the counter and said, "Henry wants you to take over the cash register this afternoon. I've got to work on the books."

"Cooking them?"

"I wish I was that slick. No, I'm just following up on some accounts that may need a little coaxing."

"A friendly reminder."

"Exactly. Do you want to get some dinner tonight before the fights? There's a pretty good burger joint a block away from the arena."

"Fine. Pick you up at six?"

"You want to drive?"

"I get restless when I'm in the passenger seat."

"You don't like somebody else deciding where you go?"

"Maybe."

"I'm at twenty-three Pastor's Walk. That's the street behind Sarge's Diner."

"I'll find it."

"See you later."

When Henry finally finished instructing Billy, he nodded "hello" to Lucas but avoided talking to him for most of the afternoon.

At about four-thirty, there wasn't a customer in sight. Lucas

poured himself a cup of coffee and took the last doughnut. Henry joined him at the counter.

"Slow day," Lucas said.

"Yes."

"You're awfully patient with Billy."

"I guess so."

"Does he remind you of yourself? When you were his age?"

"No. Why would he?"

"I don't know. He's not much like his father, is he?"

"Emily still hasn't called you?"

"She can't call me."

"What do you mean?"

"She doesn't have my phone number."

Henry ran his fingers through his hair as if he were trying to tear it out by the roots.

"Why not?"

"I don't give people my number. Don't worry. I told her to call me here. You'll be the first to know."

Lucas chewed on the stale doughnut and sipped his coffee.

Henry shifted his weight uneasily, but he didn't leave.

"Leo and I are going to St. Albans tonight. To the fights. Are you interested?"

"Why would I want to watch people hurting each other?"

Lucas nodded and sipped his coffee. Henry turned and started to walk away.

"I had that dream again. Last night."

Henry turned back toward Lucas, started to say something, but stopped himself.

"It was exactly the same. Except . . ."

Henry almost whispered, "Except . . ."

"When the preacher touched me, his hand was as cold as ice. I could feel the coldness all through me."

He paused, then added, "I thought Hell was hot."

"Some say Hell isn't fire. It's ice."

"What do you think?"

"I don't know. I don't plan to find out."

17

The Fights

Leo's house was a small, neatly furnished cottage in the section of town called the Glade.

"You've got a nice place here," Lucas said.

"It's not bad. You know, Emily still owns all the houses in the Glade. She's my landlady."

"They really sewed up this town, didn't they?"

"Big, hungry fish in a little pond. Want a beer before we go?"

"Sure."

Leo went into the kitchen and came out with two uncapped bottles of beer, then ushered Lucas into the living room.

There were a few nondescript paintings on the wall, but no photographs anywhere.

Lucas thought, *It's as if Leo has no past. Or maybe that he prefers not to remember it.*

They drank their beers in silence for a few minutes.

Then Lucas said, "I asked Henry if he wanted to join us tonight."

Leo laughed. "He's much too holy to watch a couple of guys beat the hell out of each other."

"Unless it's a match between God and the Devil."

"If I were still a betting man, I'd put my money on the Devil. I think he can beat the spread."

"Henry should hear you now. You'd be looking for another job."

Leo smiled. "He knows how I feel. But he needs me to run the place."

"Has he offered you a piece of the action?"

"I'm not interested."

"How come?"

"I can leave any time I want. I like to travel light."

"I understand that feeling."

"I'm sure you do. You've got no ties, right?"

"Right."

Leo sipped his beer, savored it and said, "You're really getting to Henry."

"Am I?"

"At first, it was all about Emily and the factory."

"I'm just giving the project a little push."

"But now there's something else going on."

"Is there?"

"What is it you want from Henry?"

"I don't want anything from him."

"And it isn't only Henry. I've played too much poker not to recognize a bluff when I see one."

"I'm not bluffing."

"Sure you are."

"I'm not a card player, Leo. I never was."

"What were you, Lucas? Really."

"What I said I was."

"Why is Henry afraid of you?"

"What makes you think he's afraid of me?"

"The way he keeps watching you. Like he's watching a bomb about to go off."

"You're imagining things."

Leo smiled, finished his beer and whispered, "Boom."

Lucas laughed. "Ready for that burger?"

When they reached St. Albans, Lucas parked his car in the virtually empty lot at the roller-skating rink/arena. Leo bought two tickets ("My treat."). Then they walked one block to the restaurant, Al's Corner, where they each had the house special with onions, and another beer. At seven forty-five, when they returned to the arena, most of the parking spots were occupied. They followed the crowd inside.

A ring had been set up in the center of the broad, high-ceilinged room. It was surrounded by rows of folding chairs, some of which were already occupied. A young man was walking up and down the aisles, selling beer. Several illuminated signs read, "NO SMOKING," but rivers of cigar and cigarette smoke streamed through the beams of the spotlights focused on the ring. A fleshy young woman in a very short black skirt, black halter top, black fishnet stockings and three-inch heels stood near the ring steps, drinking beer, laughing and waving to passers-by, greeting some by name.

Leo said, "Even in a small town like this, we've got a round-card girl."

"Nothing but the best for St. Albans."

They sat in the third row. A few minutes later, a short, wiry man in his mid-sixties wove his way through the ropes into the ring.

He was wearing a light blue shirt, red tie, blue blazer and tan slacks. He tested the portable microphone he was carrying—"one, two, three"—then said in a surprisingly deep, thick voice, "Ladies and gentlemen, good evening to you, and welcome to another big, *big* St. Albans Fight Night. I'm your ring announcer, Jimmy Jermaine."

He was greeted with half-hearted applause and cheers.

"The promoter of tonight's card is St. Albans's own Dave Hicks. The judges are Nat Brown and Stanley Watkins. Referee Bob Hayward will be the third man in the ring, and will also score the fights." (Scattered applause.) "As always, ladies and gentlemen, our generous sponsor tonight is Barclay's Beer Distributors. *Say Barclay's when you want Beer at Its Best!*" (Loud applause and cheers.)

He pointed toward the first row of seats, at the young woman in the short, black skirt and said, "Adding a touch of feminine beauty and pulchritude to the evening, our charming round-card girl tonight is the very lovely Selena Madison."

Selena turned, waved and smiled at the audience. They all greeted her enthusiastically.

"We have a terrific, action-packed card for you tonight—six potent pugilistic pairings. The main event is a tough ten-round tussle between the undefeated Connecticut heavyweight champion, hard-hitting Sammy *the Slammer* Santana" (Cheers and some boos) "and the former WB Americas heavyweight titleholder—from Philadelphia, P-A—Petey Padilla." (Boos.)

"Connecticut champion?" Leo asked. "WB Americas? Remember when there were eight weight classes and eight champions? Now, there are junior middleweights and super welterweights and who knows what else. And every fighter seems to be a champion of something or other."

"Careful, Leo. You're showing your age."

By now, most of the crowd was seated.

The first fight was a four-rounder between a local twenty-

year-old welterweight named Geoff Wallace, with a record of 6-0, and a slow-moving veteran, who was hand-picked to add a "W" to the younger man's record.

Wallace was arrogant and awkward, strutting around the ring, throwing flashy, inaccurate punches, mugging for the crowd, and wasting his energy on meaningless dance steps. His friends and family, seated in the third row on Lucas's left, cheered loudly at everything Wallace did. His opponent patiently followed him, jabbing occasionally, avoiding most of Wallace's telegraphed punches, and allowing himself to get hit now and then, so Wallace could score a few points.

The young man won a unanimous decision. His entourage cheered him loudly and left *en masse*.

Leo nudged Lucas with his elbow. "Look who's here."

Sarge and Luther were coming down the aisle, aiming at two of the empty seats vacated by Wallace's friends and family.

"Hi, Sarge. Luther," Leo said. "Didn't know you were coming tonight."

As they sat down, Sarge smiled and said, "Thanks for saving us such good seats."

Luther frowned, as if he suspected foul play.

The second bout was a dull six-rounder. The boxers were out-of-shape middleweights who were too tired to throw punches after the third round. The crowd booed as they waltzed around the ring, gasping for air and yearning for the final bell.

"You know, I fought in the Golden Gloves for a couple of years, in New York, when I was a teenager," Sarge said. "The first year, I actually reached the semifinals."

"And the guy who beat you turned out to be Rocky Marciano?" Leo said.

Sarge laughed.

"No, but he might as well have been. He was a big black

kid with a hell of a punch. I knew he'd knocked out a couple of guys, but I was pretty cocky. I won the first round, jabbing, moving, landing a couple of shots. The crowd loved me. In between rounds, my trainer said, 'Be careful, this kid can hit. Don't let him catch up with you. Keep moving to your right, and stay off the ropes.' In the second round, I did what he told me—for about a minute—and then I decided to land a couple of big shots. I got off my bicycle, started to throw a right hand—and the next thing I know, I'm flat on my back, bells are ringing in my ears, the lights are dancing around like the fucking Rockettes and I'm history."

"Live and learn," Leo said.

"Did you do any better the next year?" Lucas asked.

"No. I wasn't a novice any more and I came up against guys who were a little older, and a lot more experienced."

Leo ordered four beers from the wandering vendor and passed them along.

"I guess your boxing came in handy when you became a cop," Lucas said.

"The last thing a cop wants to do is fight."

Luther nodded and agreed: "Damn straight."

"We're not Superman. You always run into guys who are bigger and tougher than you. What are you going to do: shoot them all?"

"What *do* you do?"

"You stay calm. You speak softly. You try to take the edge off things. If there's a fight, you break it up. If there's one guy who's really the problem, you try to isolate him."

Luther added, "And if it's a husband and wife going at it, you call for back-up!"

They all laughed.

Lucas sipped his beer and asked, "You retired early, didn't you? How come?"

"Too much stress for me, and for Ellie. Being a cop in Pennington is about as exciting as kissing your sister. (No offense, Luther.) But where I was, in the Bronx, it was a whole different world. After a while, if somebody was black or Puerto Rican, I didn't believe him, or trust him. It didn't matter who it was, even if it was a kid, or a woman, or an old lady, or even a priest, for Chrissake. I kept getting more and more suspicious of everybody. I couldn't do it any more."

"He was a great cop," Luther said. "Decorated three or four times."

"I just couldn't do it any more. And I had enough time on the force to retire. So here I am."

Leo smiled: "And if you had won the Golden Gloves, you might have been the heavyweight champion!"

Lucas said, "I'll drink to that."

By the time the main event began, they had polished off two more rounds of beer.

Sammy *the Slammer* Santana was a tall, solid, 200-pounder. His opponent, Petey Padilla, was a black fighter, a few inches shorter, a few pounds heavier, with a compact, puncher's build— long, sinewy arms, broad shoulders and a thick chest. Santana was a serious young fighter, who listened carefully to his manager's instructions. Padilla kept looking around the arena with the easy confidence of a veteran, sizing up the crowd and smiling at the round-card girl.

Santana's record was a perfect 17-0, with ten knock-outs. Padilla had 32 victories, 12 defeats, and 20 knock-outs.

"Santana better watch out," Sarge said. "I've seen Padilla. He's good."

In the first round, Santana boxed cautiously, throwing solid jabs and moving well. Padilla was in no hurry. He moved just enough to stay out of range of Santana's occasional right hand.

In the second round, Santana became more aggressive, jabbing and then moving in with a straight right or a left hook off the jab. Again, Padilla ducked or slipped every punch except one left hook toward the end of the round. Going back to his corner, Santana was clearly pleased.

"The spider and the fly," Sarge said.

"Which is which?" Luther asked.

Sarge smiled.

In the third round, Santana quickened the pace. He kept moving forward, jabbing quickly and following up with two- and three-punch combinations. Padilla picked off some of the punches with his gloves, or ducked under them, or pulled back just enough to make Santana miss. With a minute to go in the round, Santana began to get overconfident. He trapped Padilla in a corner of the ring, jabbed twice and then swung a looping right hand. Padilla ducked under the punch, pivoted and snapped a left hook over Santana's right, hitting him on the temple. Santana dropped his hands. His right knee trembled. His mouth fell open, as if he were trying to think of something to say. His eyes stared at something out of range. Padilla slipped out of the corner as Santana fell onto his back, his head bouncing off the canvas floor.

The referee didn't have to finish the count. The crowd was silent. Santana's corner men came into the ring to revive him. The referee raised Padilla's hand. The ring announcer told everyone what they already knew. Padilla smiled at the round-card girl.

After the fights, they stopped into Al's Corner for one more beer.

Leo said, "You were right about Padilla, Sarge. The spider and the fly."

"That's how young fighters learn. That's how I learned I shouldn't be a fighter."

Lucas asked Sarge, "Do you ever miss being a cop?"

"No. If I ever start to think about it, I remember—well, I just remember."

"It sounds like there's one particular thing you remember."

Sarge nodded. "Yeah, maybe."

"Never mind that," Luther said.

Sarge looked at Lucas and nodded again.

"I picked up this kid—nineteen or twenty—for selling drugs. He was high as a kite when I grabbed him. And he was holding a pretty big stash. He was fingered by one of the snitches we had on the payroll."

Luther interrupted: "Never mind, Sarge. It doesn't matter now."

"The trial was a joke. It took a couple of hours. I was the only witness they needed. The kid got a shit-load of years. His sister comes up to me after the trial. She's crying, of course, and she says her brother uses but he doesn't sell. She says the snitch had it in for him. Something about a girl. I told her to work a little harder and come up with a new story, one I hadn't heard a thousand times before.

"About six months later, she comes into the station. She tells me that her brother killed himself. She says it's my fault that he's dead. I tell her that it's not my fault that her brother was a hophead and a pusher. She says I should check out the snitch's story if I want to know the truth. I tell her 'goodbye'."

"But you checked out the story?" Lucas asked.

"Yeah. On my own time."

Sarge finished his beer.

"She was right. The kid had taken the snitch's girlfriend. I tracked down the girl. She told me the snitch had bragged to her about how he set the kid up."

Sarge looked down into his empty beer glass.

"Mistakes happen," Luther said.

"But I started to wonder how many other mistakes I had made."

"That's a hell of a burden, isn't it, Sarge?" Lucas asked.

"Yeah."

Luther didn't agree: "You know how many bad asses you got off the street? How many lives did that save?"

"He may be right, Sarge."

"I hope to God he's right, Lucas."

"Right or wrong, it's time to go home," Luther said. "Come on, Sarge."

On the way back to Pennington, Leo fell asleep, slumped down in the seat.

Lucas thought about what Sarge had said.

It's over with Sarge, just like that, just in one night. He doesn't hide his sins.

Lucas was tying up the loose ends quickly, too quickly. He didn't have to work very hard at it. It was so easy finding the hidden places, the dark places. Or was he just getting better at it? He wouldn't have to stay in Pennington much longer.

But he could still see Beth's eyes. His wife's empty eyes. Diana's blood, staining the snow.

Leo moaned a couple of times. He was awake now, but he was feeling the effects of the beer much more than Lucas was.

"I think I'm beginning to understand your game, Lucas."

"Are you?"

"Always asking questions, never answering them. Getting inside people." He tried to imitate Lucas's voice: "'That's a hell of a burden, isn't it, Sarge?'"

"I guess I'm just curious."

"No, it's more than that."

He leaned over and looked at Lucas.

"Digging, always digging."

"Like I said, I guess I'm just curious."

"I thought Henry was the one who's in love with sin. But you may have a worse case."

He closed his eyes.

"Did you come here to condemn us?" he asked. "Or to forgive us?"

He looked over at Lucas, angrily for a moment. And then the anger faded and he seemed very calm and relaxed.

"Tell you what I'm gonna do, Lucas. I'm going to save you the trouble of all that digging. I'm going to offer you my truth on a silver platter, free of charge. My truth."

"You don't have to tell me anything."

"But I want to. Christ, I want to tell someone."

He closed his eyes again, but they shifted back and forth, as if he were watching a private movie screen.

"I told you I was a player. I kept traveling from town to town, from game to game. I made money. Lots of money. I tell you, man, it was a good life. And there were plenty of sweet, pretty young things along the way, too. Yeah, it was a good life. Then I met Julia, and she wasn't just sweet and pretty. She was special. But she didn't like the life I was living. Or the people I hung out with. She didn't like them at all. I tried, but I couldn't let her go. So we got married and we settled down in New York City—in Queens. It was a mistake.

"I got a job doing some dull office shit, making a living, grinding it out, the same shit every day. I hated it. I began to hate

myself and I began to hate Julia. Finally, I told her I had to get back to the life. But I said it would be like a business trip, like I was a traveling salesman, or something. A few weeks here, a few weeks there, and then I'd come home with a pocket full of money. She wasn't happy about it, but I didn't let her stop me.

"Besides, by that time, she had someone else to make her happy. We had a son, Thomas, a beautiful boy. Thank God, he didn't look like me. He looked just like his mom. He was four when I went back on the road. It worked out pretty well. I spent enough time at home with Thomas and Julia, but I kept doing what I loved to do and I made lots of money. We lived well. And when Thomas was in his teens, I started to school him, to teach him what I knew. Julia and I had plenty of arguments about that. But I thought it would be good for the boy.

"Right after his sixteenth birthday, I was traveling out in the Midwest. Thomas and a friend of his got into a game—with some people he shouldn't have been playing with. He was dealing and he decided to try one of the tricks I had taught him, probably just to see if he could get away with it. He couldn't. He didn't."

He opened his eyes and sat up straight, staring at the road ahead. The private movie was still on the screen.

"These were real players. One of them shot him. Killed him. My son. Julia's son. She didn't even call me to tell me about it. I missed his funeral. I was out in Chicago. When I came back, she had already packed up everything to move out. She was waiting there to tell me what had happened. And then she said, 'I pray that you'll burn in Hell for what you did.' That's the last thing she ever said to me.

"After that, I wandered around for a while, did some heavy drinking. Never played cards again. Took what jobs I could get. It was really nothing new to me: I was used to being a stranger in

town. When I came to Pennington, I asked Henry for a day's work. That was six—almost seven years ago."

He was silent for a minute or two.

"I can still see Julia's face. And I know she's praying, every day, that I burn in Hell. I can still see that little boy the day he was born, that beautiful little boy. And I can see him when he was growing tall and handsome. His smile. His grave. Her prayers have been answered."

Leo said, "That's my truth. You don't have to dig for it."

He closed his eyes and didn't say another word.

When Lucas returned to his apartment, he tried to sleep, but couldn't. He paced slowly back and forth in the living room. He got a cold beer from the refrigerator, and continued to pace.

The Santana-Padilla boxing match that night had reminded him of another fight, on a New Year's Eve almost four years ago.

He was at his Manhattan office with Diana. They had stopped off on the way to their house up in the Vermont mountains—they called it their "cabin in the sky"—to pick up some reports they might read over the holidays. Diana was a beautiful, brilliant financial whiz kid, hard-edged and ambitious, twenty-five years younger than Lucas. She worked closely with him, and lived with him. She never asked about marriage because she didn't know that he had divorced his wife. (No one else, not even Beth, knew that.)

The office was on the fortieth floor of a glass-walled tower near Central Park. It had just begun to snow and, to Lucas, the flakes falling past the brightly-lit windows looked like shooting stars.

He told Diana his time at the company was almost over. He was planning to move on, and he wanted her to move with him.

"Whither thou goest . . ." she said, and kissed him.

Someone shouted, "I didn't know that sharks could fall in love!"

It was Tim McNeill, the former CEO of the company, the man Lucas had replaced. McNeill obviously had an early start on welcoming in the new year.

He walked unsteadily toward Lucas and said, "Congratulations! In just eighteen months, you've managed to kill my company."

"I saved your fucking company, Tim, which is more than *you* could do. Look at the stock price. Hey, you should thank me. Your options are going to be worth a fortune."

"How many people did you fire? Good people! Thousands of them. No more pensions, no more benefits."

"You sound like a union man, Tim. That's not what the Street wants. They always love what I do, because I push the stock price up. So they make their money, and I make mine. And you'll make yours, too."

"You lousy bastard!"

McNeill threw a wild, roundhouse right at Lucas, who ducked under it easily, shifted his weight and hit him in the temple with a hard left hook, just the way Padilla had hit Santana. The result was the same.

A few hours later, Lucas was driving through a snowstorm on a twisting, icy road in Vermont. The smooth, pulsing beat of a Modern-Jazz-Quartet CD erased the howl of the wind and the steady hum of the windshield wipers. Neither he nor Diana was wearing a seat belt. ("Seat belts are for losers," she always said.)

Diana had brought along a thermos bottle filled with premixed Manhattans, which didn't take them long to finish.

"We'll be there in a little while," Lucas said, "nice and warm by the fire."

The knuckles of his left hand still ached ("Damnit, McNeill has a hard head!"), but the pain was like a distant island lost in the mists of a warm, hazy sea. He was swimming in that misty warmth, deeper and deeper. He was already feeling the heat of the fireplace at their cabin, and her heat, too.

Diana sang, "Let it snow, let it snow, let it snow . . ."

He nodded and smiled at her.

Suddenly, around a sharp turn, he faced the bright headlights of an oncoming car. His reactions were a shade too slow. Overcompensating, he moved the wheel too quickly. He avoided the other car, but he skidded, spun around, hit a retaining wall, slid back onto the road and off again, and plowed into a stand of pine trees. The roof of the car was torn off like the lid of a tin can. An instant later, he was thrown through the frozen, black night air, landing in a thick snow bank. He lay still for a minute or two or three, wondering if he would be able to move. Cautiously, carefully, he felt his arms and legs and chest. Nothing seemed to be broken. Blood ran down his face from cuts on his scalp. He had survived virtually unhurt.

He was dizzy and confused, but he managed to get to his feet. He looked for Diana. The car had been stopped by a massive tree. Its headlights were still alive, so he could see Diana, who had also been thrown from the car, in a clearing a few yards away. She was lying on her back in the snow. He struggled to reach her, gasping for breath, exhaling huge vapor clouds.

She still looked beautiful. Her long, dark hair framed her face softly. A streak of blood stained her forehead and ran onto the snow, like a crimson waterfall. Her eyes were open, but they didn't blink as the snowflakes fell onto them and melted.

He crouched beside her, shivered in the wet cold, wiped some of the blood away from her face, stroked her hair, watched the snow's shooting stars flutter in the glare of the headlights.

The white-shrouded trees looked down at them silently, dispassionately.

Like the souls of the saved looking down at the souls of the damned.

He didn't know how much time had passed when he heard car engines, voices. He saw headlights, the tight beam of a flashlight. An ambulance for him. A hearse for her?

If you have enough money, it's easy to buy off the local cops. It's easy to disappear. Money makes everything easy.

He couldn't remember much about the next year. He went on binge after binge, drying out for a while; then drinking again, and repeating the cycle, over and over. Weeks and months streamed by quickly, darkly, unremembered. Finally, he checked himself into a hospital, where he dried out and stayed sober, and told the young female psychiatrist and the middle-aged male psychiatrist what he thought they wanted to hear: how he yearned for his dead father, hated his mother, hurt his wife, neglected his daughter. They talked to him gently, firmly, coaxed him, guided him, believed that he believed them. They gave him pills that calmed him down. When he felt calm enough without the pills, he told them that he was cured, thanked them, checked himself out, bought a second-hand car, packed a bag, and began to travel from place to place, across the country.

Wherever he went, whether he stayed for a week or a month or more, he searched for the hidden places, the dark places, the truth behind the lies that people told. Because he was sure he had discovered the cure for his illness, and it wasn't what the psychiatrists thought it was. All he had to do was prove to himself that even the good people, the decent people, were as guilty, as sinful as he was. That everyone has something to hide.

Lucas finished the beer. He lay down on the couch in the living room and fell asleep.

Again, the rose garden. Thousands of rose bushes all around him, packed tightly against each other, towering over his head. Wingthorn rose bushes. The branches were stiff and purplish, with small, dark green leaves and tiny, white, four-petalled flowers. All the branches were covered with large, blood-red thorns—thorns that were attached to the branches by translucent, bloody membranes. He was running on a narrow, twisting, dirt path. He was naked and barefoot. His bare arms brushed against the bushes on each side of him. Every bush he touched pierced his flesh with its thorns and then withered and blackened and died. His blood, thin and pink and watery, streamed down his arms and dripped off his fingertips. He looked behind him as he ran. He was leaving a clear trail: withered, dead rose bushes and, on the dirt path, two muddy streams of blood. He could hear the footsteps getting closer and closer. He smiled. Whatever was hunting him could track him easily, no matter how long he ran, or how far he traveled. And it was catching up to him. That was a comforting thought. He kept running.

Lucas opened his eyes. Whatever it was, he wished it would catch him soon.

18

Just a Curious Small-Town Guy

Lucas woke up very early on Saturday morning. He had slept for only a few hours. His head ached and his mouth was dry.

He sat up in bed and leaned back against the headboard, staring at the wall. He felt cold and hollow, as if his body had been drained of blood.

He wasn't surprised at the way he felt. In other places, other towns, it had ended this way, he had felt this way.

If I do this a thousand times, will it be any different?

Maybe the psychiatrists were right. Maybe they could cure him. Maybe not. That almost didn't matter to him any more. It was as if the search had become more important than what he found.

He would play the end game here, nothing more than that. Play the game, dream of the rose garden. And then find another place, other sinners, other sins.

But Katharine, his wife, would still be lost to him, and so would Beth. Diana would still be dead.

And if he told her what he was, Margot would be lost to him, too.

Leo quit playing his game. Can I quit mine?
Henry. Emily. The end game.
Then back on the road.

At the garden center, Leo was obviously hung over, but he smiled a quiet, comfortable "good morning."

Lucas poured himself a cup of black coffee and joined Leo and Henry at the counter.

Henry was tight-lipped and uneasy.

"If Emily doesn't call you soon . . ."

"She will."

"She's having her fun."

"I'll bet she is," Lucas said. "And how are you this morning, Leo?"

"Oh, am I in town?" Leo sighed.

Lucas smiled.

Henry asked, "You went to the fights last night?"

Lucas nodded.

"I don't understand how you can enjoy something like that."

"I guess we're just sinners."

"I guess we are," Leo said, raising his coffee cup as if he were proposing a toast.

Henry frowned.

"Pride is the father of sin."

Lucas groaned.

"Henry, please. It's too early in the morning."

Henry shook his head and frowned again.

An hour later, and an hour late, Billy Miles, Jr., arrived. Lucas was setting up a display of gardening tools at the far end of

the room, so he couldn't hear the conversation between Henry and Billy. But the scene was a silent replica of others he had witnessed: Billy, hostile and edgy; Henry, reserved, patient, almost deferential. From this distance, Lucas noticed for the first time how closely Billy's body language mirrored Henry's.

The end game.

At a few minutes after eleven o'clock, Lucas was helping Henry unload fifty-pound sacks of grass seed from a delivery truck when Leo called out to him, "Emily Grant's on the phone."

"Be right there."

Henry followed him in. The telephone receiver was on the counter. Henry stood a few feet from him.

Lucas picked up the receiver.

"Hello, Emily. How are you?"

"Better."

"I guess that means Jeanette is back in the fold."

"So it seems."

Her voice sounded aggressive again.

"Does that take me off the hook as a bad influence?"

"I'm still reserving judgment."

"What more can I do?"

She laughed.

"How about giving me your phone number?"

"And reveal my final mystery? Not yet."

She paused, then said, "I'm calling about the factory."

"What have you decided to do?"

"I've thought about the proposal, and your suggestions. I've discussed everything with my lawyers and my accountant. I'll let you know what my decision is tomorrow. Come to the Grange for lunch in the afternoon. After church. At two."

"Somehow I can't picture you in church."

"Why not?"

"Answering to a higher authority? That doesn't sound like you."

"I'm just covering my bets."

"Said like a true believer."

"I'll see you tomorrow."

"Yes, tomorrow."

When he hung up, Henry leaned close to him and asked, "Well? What'd she say?"

"She'll tell me tomorrow. At lunch."

"How did she sound? Positive? Negative?"

"She's never that obvious."

Henry sighed.

"I'm going over to Sarge's for a while," he said. "I'll be back before you close. Lucas, get Billy to help you finish unloading the truck."

After he left, Leo asked, "Do you think she'll make the deal?"

"Probably."

"They'll really owe you—Henry and the others."

"It won't work that way. Whatever they get, they'll say it isn't enough. And they'll blame me. They'll say they could have done better."

"But she wasn't even talking to them."

"Leo, when you help people, they end up hating you."

"That doesn't make sense."

"They feel you've showed them up. It's the fastest way I know to make enemies."

"Well, you'll make the enemies, and they'll make the money."

"I wonder if it's really the money that matters to them."

"You've got to be kidding."

"It won't be enough to really change their lives. I think they just want to win—to come out ahead of Emily just once."

"I know the feeling. Winning tastes good. I miss that more than anything else about the life." His eyes narrowed as he remembered. "Reading the cards, reading the odds, reading the faces. Knowing what you're reading, and how to use it. Outthinking and outlasting everyone at the table."

"I miss that, too."

Leo smiled.

"Miss it? Isn't that what you're doing here?"

"Not exactly."

"What exactly are you doing?"

"Just looking for the truth."

Leo laughed.

"Amen," he said.

Henry got back to the center just in time to close it.

Lucas invited Leo to his apartment for a beer—"the hair of the dog."

"It may not be worth your while. I don't have any more secrets."

Lucas smiled.

"That's for me to decide."

"I probably shouldn't, but . . ."

A few minutes later, they were sitting on the patio, savoring the cool taste of beer in the warmth of the afternoon sun.

Leo wondered, "When this factory deal is finally settled, one way or the other, what the hell are Henry and Ernie and Billy going to worry about?"

"I'm sure they'll find something."

"What are you getting out of the deal?"

"Not a penny."

"Okay, no money. Then what else?"

"I enjoy being the deal maker."

"Even in this crummy little town?"

"A deal is a deal."

"You like to be the one who makes it happen?"

"You said you miss winning. I miss it sometimes, too."

Leo shook his head.

"I'm still not sure where you're coming from, Lucas. I still can't put all the pieces together. But that's okay. I get the feeling you're not long for this town."

"You're right."

Joey came out onto the patio. He was wearing a blue blazer and tan slacks, a light blue shirt and a red tie.

Just like the ring announcer in St. Albans.

"Do you want a beer?" Lucas asked.

"No, thanks."

"Going to work?"

"Yeah. Then it's off to the races tonight," Joey added, without enthusiasm.

"Who's the lucky girl this weekend?"

"What difference does it make?"

Lucas smiled. "You sound like you're getting tired of women."

"Shit, I've always been tired of women. But I need them."

"That's life, I guess."

"I guess." Joey paused for a moment, then asked, "What's going on with you and Fay?"

"Not much lately."

"You have an argument, or something?"

"You could say that. We can't seem to agree about anything any more."

"She's a pain in the ass. She's never made it easy for me. And what the hell is she doing in Providence?"

"I have no idea."

"When's she coming back?"

"Tonight, I think. Or tomorrow."

"Pain in the ass. I better get to work."

After he had gone, Leo said, "Poor bastard."

"Yeah. He keeps doing the same thing, over and over again, and he doesn't know why."

"Don't we all? I remember what it was like. I was hooked on women, too."

"Not any more?"

"Not any more. Not at all."

"You're still a young man, Leo. You may change your mind."

"I may."

Leo began to say something, hesitated, then began again.

"Why did you come to Pennington, Lucas?"

"At the time, it seemed like a place where I could settle down."

"Come on, that's not true, is it? I've heard the story about you being a small-town guy, and all that crap. And it is crap, isn't it?"

"I *am* from Shelby, Pennsylvania. I was born there and grew up there. Scout's honor."

"But you're from a lot of other places since then. And you're on your way to somewhere else. Why stop here?"

"Why not?"

Leo shook his head.

"I had too much to drink last night."

"No kidding."

"But I'm not sorry I told you about—what happened."

"You don't have to worry about me telling anyone else."

"I'm not worried. But it was really important to you that I tell you, wasn't it? And you made sure that Sarge talked about why he quit the police force. I'll bet you're doing the same kind of thing with other people here. But why does any of it matter to you?"

"I told you: I'm just curious."

"Just a curious small-town guy," Leo said, raising his beer bottle in a toast. "Down the hatch."

19

Keeping the Faith

Joey didn't come home on Saturday night but, a few minutes before ten o'clock, Fay did. Lucas was certain she wanted to tell him why she had gone to Providence, but he assumed she would wait until the next day. He didn't mind waiting: she was already out of reach, so he was in no hurry to hear her story. Besides, he had more important business tonight.

At about ten-thirty, he left the apartment and walked to Henry's house. The lights were on in one of the rooms on the second floor. Lucas rang the bell.

After a minute or two, the porch light went on. When Henry opened the door, he didn't seem to recognize Lucas at first.

"I'm sorry to bother you so late, Henry, but I've got to talk to you."

Henry was wearing pajamas and a bathrobe. He was holding one of the red-covered copies of *The New Testament*.

"Now? I'd rather not . . ."

Lucas interrupted him: "You're the only one who can help me."

208

He pushed past Henry, into the foyer.

"Help you?"

Reluctantly, he closed the door behind him and gestured for Lucas to follow him into the living room. Henry switched on an overhead light and sat in an armchair. He put the book on his lap and folded his arms across it, as if he were protecting it. Lucas sat on the sofa.

"What kind of help do you think I can give you?"

Lucas leaned forward.

"I keep having that dream, that same dream. And it keeps getting worse."

"I can't help you. I don't know anything about dreams."

"But I know who the minister is. The one who's preaching in the empty church. The one who reaches out to me."

"I can't help you."

"He has red hair. He's preaching the faith. I know him. He knows me."

Henry's fingers gripped the spine of the book tightly.

"I don't . . ."

"The minister is you, Henry."

"Don't be ridiculous."

"It's you, Henry. It is."

Henry stood up, holding *The New Testament* in front of him, like a shield.

"I'm—I'm not a minister."

"You're there, every night," Lucas whispered, looking up at Henry. "Every night. In that dark, empty church."

"That isn't me."

"I'm afraid to go to sleep. You've got to leave me alone."

Henry sat down.

He took a deep breath and said, "This has nothing to do with

me. I don't know why you're having this dream. I don't know why I'm in it—why you think I'm in it."

"You were going to be a minister, weren't you?"

"Yes."

"You were at the seminary?"

"Yes, I was."

"But you left. Why?"

"That's my business, not yours."

"I was at your Bible study class. You have the calling. I could see that."

"I do what I can."

"But in my dream, you've lost your faith."

"I haven't lost my faith. I've never lost my faith."

"In my dream . . ."

"I have nothing to do with your dreams. I'm sorry, but I can't help you."

He stood up again, as if the conversation were over. Lucas ignored the gesture.

"If you never lost your faith, why did you leave the seminary?"

"I don't have to explain myself to you. And I don't want to talk about this again."

Lucas sighed.

"I'm sorry I bothered you."

"So am I."

Lucas followed Henry to the door.

"Goodnight, Henry."

Henry didn't answer.

Early the next morning—a muggy, overcast Sunday morning—Fay knocked at Lucas's door.

She was wearing a sweat suit. So was he.

"I see you're ready for our morning walk. Let's go," she said.

They were silent until they approached the Cascades. Then Lucas asked, "How was your trip to Providence?"

"It was just what I needed."

"What you needed?"

"A way out of here."

"You could have left a long time ago."

"I wasn't ready. But you changed that."

"If you say so."

"I've been thinking of writing a short story about you. I used to try to write fiction. I even had a story published a long time ago—in one of those little magazines that pays you with ten copies of itself."

"Why would you want to write about me?"

"Don't be so modest. You know you're an interesting character: a mysterious stranger who stirs things up in a small town. He says he's searching for the truth. As it turns out, he's only interested in finding the bad kind of truth. What is he up to? What does he want?"

"How does the story end?"

"I'm not sure. A writer has to understand a character's motivation. That's what makes a story worthwhile. And in your case, I'm going to have to make it all up."

"I can't wait to read it. I'd love to know what makes me tick."

She smiled, but didn't say anything.

Heavy, gray clouds moved sluggishly across the sky, like a veil over the sun. The woods and the grass took on the same gray color, as if the Cascades were in mourning.

Fay said, "You're right. I should have left Pennington years ago."

"Leaving all your sins behind you?"

"I'm not a sinner, Lucas. I just had some bad luck and it got the best of me."

"You're letting yourself off lightly."

"And who are you: God? I thought Henry had the vengeance market cornered."

"You don't believe in God anyway, do you?"

"Not if He's like you. What ever happened to forgiveness?"

"It's not that easy to come by."

"I don't need your forgiveness. Or Henry's. Or God's, for that matter. I can forgive myself."

"Do you want me to move out?"

"You don't have to. I'm leaving."

"Running away."

"You could call it that. I wouldn't. At a Library Association meeting a few years ago, I met a woman who's the corporate librarian for a company in Providence. An insurance company. We've kept in touch. She's in her early sixties and she'd like to retire soon. She's asked me—more than once—to come work for her, so I could take over her job when she leaves. A couple of days ago, I went to see her. I told her I would take her offer, if it was still open."

She began to walk more quickly, as if she were starting the return trip to Providence on foot. He kept pace with her.

"You can leave Pennington," he said, "but that doesn't mean you'll leave everything behind you."

"I already have."

"I don't believe that."

She stopped and turned to face him.

"Believe it, Lucas. I'm sorry to disappoint you, but I'm not a repentant sinner—or any other kind of sinner."

She began to walk again, but he didn't follow.

"When are you leaving?"

"In a few days. Joey can have the house. He's your new landlord. I'm staying with Anne (that's her name) until I can find an apartment."

She had won. And as he watched her walk away, he wondered why her victory didn't disappoint him.

She turned, looked back at him, smiled and said, "Hey, Lucas: keep the faith."

20

Call Me

When Lucas arrived at the Grange, Cameron ushered him into the conservatory.

The air in the high-ceilinged, glass-walled expanse was moist, and heavy with the scent of flowers. The sun was still masked by dense clouds; the light in the room gray and cold. The walls had become almost translucent: reflected images from the interior floated across the landscape like ghosts.

Emily was seated at a white, wrought iron table that reminded Lucas of the bench in front of Margot's house.

"Good afternoon, Lucas."

He sat down across from her.

"Jeanette won't be joining us. Would you like a drink? Some wine, perhaps?"

"I would prefer coffee."

Emily gestured to Cameron, who served a cup to each of them.

"Cameron, we'll be having lunch in twenty minutes. We won't need you until then."

He nodded and left.

"You look a little under the weather, Lucas. Not feeling well?"

"I'm fine. Just a little tired."

"Of Pennington? Of your nervous friends? Or of me?"

"Nothing that dramatic. I just haven't been getting enough sleep lately."

"Is that so? I wonder if I can believe anything you say."

Lucas smiled.

"You're not the only one who feels that way."

"I suppose the Three Musketeers are still wondering why you worked so hard to win me over."

"Have I won you over?"

Emily sipped her coffee, looked out at the dreary day and nodded.

"It wasn't just you, of course."

"Of course."

"My marketing vice president loves the idea of a retail store where he—where we could test new lines, new ideas. I suppose he's right."

"I suppose he is."

"Do you know what I'm calling my little store?"

"I won't even try to guess."

It was Emily's turn to smile.

"I'm calling it *Emily's Place*."

"That might be a better name for the whole mall."

"Wouldn't Billy and Henry and Ernie just love that?"

They both laughed.

"No, it's going to be the Schuyler Shopping Center. Permanently. That's part of the sales agreement. And I'll retain a thirty-percent interest in it. Permanently."

"If the buyers will agree to that."

"If they don't, there's no deal."

"Have you weighed in on the finders' fee?"

"No. I don't care what they get, as long as I don't have to pay it."

"I wonder if any of them will take the money and run."

"They won't leave Pennington. It's not a lack of money that keeps them here, it's a lack of courage. And what keeps you here, Lucas?"

"The pleasure of your company."

"Really? Not your lady friend, the librarian?"

"She's not very friendly any more. In fact, she's leaving town in a couple of days. Going to Providence. She's landed a new job there."

"You wore out your welcome pretty quickly, didn't you?"

"I guess I'm not as charming as I thought I was."

"You're not charming at all. But you *are* very attractive. Twenty years ago—well, maybe twenty-five—you would have been just my cup of tea."

"I'm flattered."

Emily smiled at Lucas seductively. "I think we would have made quite a team."

"I don't doubt it."

"But that's another story."

She finished her coffee and put the cup down decisively, as if she were writing *The End* on the last page of a story.

"My lawyers have drawn up a contract and I've signed two copies. I'll give them to you after lunch. The rest is up to—the boys."

Lucas took her cue and changed the subject.

"Are any of your roses—the new ones you developed—in the conservatory?"

"You don't give a damn about flowers."

"But I'll bet that you'd love to show them off."

"Since when are you so anxious to please me? Why the sudden change in tactics?"

"You make it sound like we're at war."

"Aren't we?"

"What do you and I have to fight about?"

She studied him for a moment before she said, "Jeanette?"

"That sounded more like a question than an answer."

"She's more like a question than an answer. She is always out of reach."

"At her age, who isn't?"

"Why is she so interested in you?"

"I'm an outsider. She hasn't known me all her life. And I'm not afraid of her grandmother."

Emily nodded. "She doesn't take after her father or her mother. Not at all, thank God! She takes after me."

"Have you told her that?"

"I don't have to."

Lucas wondered if that was true; and if that made Jeanette even lonelier.

Cameron soon returned to serve lunch: grilled salmon with mixed vegetables, and a dry white wine.

They ate quietly, comfortably, as if they had taken a mutual vow of silence. Afterward, Emily gave Lucas two copies of the sales contract in an official Schuyler Enterprises manila envelope.

"If and when the papers are signed, call me," she said.

"I'll let you know."

She pursed her lips. "Unless you'd rather give me your phone number, so *I* can call *you*."

He shook his head.

She smiled and said, "Bastard."

Emily told Cameron to see Lucas to the front door. She remained seated.

217

Jeanette met him in the foyer.

"I'll walk with you to your car," she said.

Though she spoke softly, she seemed angry.

"I didn't drive here."

"Then I'll walk you to the gate."

"I doubt if your grandmother would approve."

"Let me worry about that."

When they reached the gate, Jeanette put her hand on his arm.

"Don't leave yet, Mr. Murdoch. I've got something to tell you."

She watched him opaquely, coolly.

"Should I be worried?"

"Definitely." She smiled her half-smile. "I said I would find out who you are. It took a lot of hard work, but it paid off."

"I'm not surprised."

"The Internet is a great tool. If you know how to use it."

"Please don't keep me in suspense."

"Why not? It's more fun that way."

There was no fun in her voice.

"The first problem I ran into was how to spell your name. I started with M-u-r-d-o-c-h. I turned up some interesting characters, but none of them were you. So I tried 'Murdock' with a 'k.'"

"Any luck with that?"

"Not right away. Because I thought Lucas was your first name."

"But you didn't get discouraged."

"Not at all. I just started checking all the references to Murdock. That took a long time, but I'm young. I've got plenty of time."

"Obviously."

"Then I found a seven-year-old *Business Week* article, and there you were. I wasn't sure, at first, because the photograph didn't look like you. This Murdock had long, dark hair and a beard. But he had your face—your eyes."

"I'm not convinced."

"I am. His name—your name—is Max Murdock."

"Max?"

"A *Forbes Magazine* story called you 'To-the-Max Murdock' because (and I quote) you 'take no prisoners.'"

"I must have been a very unpleasant guy."

"That's putting it mildly."

Lucas smiled. "You're right, Jeanette. I was Max Murdock. I changed the spelling of my name because the 'k' made it harder, tougher. Nice touch, I thought."

"Charming."

"When a company was in trouble, I would take it over and turn it around. I was very good at that."

"They said you were a 'union-buster'."

"Sometimes I was. I did whatever worked."

"I can see why you and grandmother get along so well."

"Yes, I understand her."

"Four years ago, Max Murdock disappeared."

"I didn't want to be Max any more. I dropped him off somewhere on a dark road in the middle of the night. I took my mother's maiden name for my first name."

"What about Max's wife and daughter?"

"Ex-wife. Ex-daughter."

The veil over her eyes dissolved into tears.

"You and grandmother. The perfect pair."

"Jeanette, I'm not Max."

"I thought . . ."

She didn't say what she thought.

He reached out his hand to wipe away her tears, but she pulled away from him.

"Believe me, Jeanette. I'm *Lucas* Murdoch now."

"I thought you could help me."

"How?"

"I can't stay here any more. With her."

"What can I do?"

"She'll never let me go. You escaped. How can I escape?"

He reached out again and, this time, she let him brush the tears from her cheeks.

He said, "You have to make her want you to go."

"How can I do that? She doesn't care how I feel."

"It's how *she* feels that matters. You have to hurt her."

"She can't be hurt."

"You have to find a way."

"Is that Lucas speaking, or Max?"

"There is no Max."

"She can't be hurt," Jeanette repeated, more softly, as if to herself.

"Here is my phone number," Lucas said. "Can you remember that?"

She repeated the number.

"You're the only one in this town who knows that number. Write it down. Call me if you need me. Any time."

"She can't be hurt."

"Think about it. Think about what matters to her."

"Why did you come to Pennington?"

"It's just one stop on the road."

"To where?"

"Remember: call me if you need me."

21

The Bar None

Lucas didn't go back to his apartment. Instead, he walked to the Cascades and followed a familiar path to the waterfall. He stood on the stone bridge and watched the current flow beneath him and drop twenty feet into the riverbed below.

He thought how easy it would be if he could move through life the way the water moved, never having to make a choice, never having to regret where he came from, or imagine where he was going.

He wondered what Beth would say about his relationship to Jeanette.

Too little, too late, with the wrong girl?

He had told Jeanette to call him, but what could he say if she did? What could he do for her? What had he done for Beth?

He reached into his pocket for his phone. He thought for a moment, and decided to call Henry at home.

Sunday afternoon, the Sabbath: the perfect time to tell him the good news.

"Hello?"

"Henry, it's Lucas."

"What did she say?"

"She's agreed to sell. With some conditions. And she won't negotiate. It's take it or leave it."

"What conditions?"

"She'll keep a third of the ownership. It'll be called the Schuyler Shopping Center. And she'll have a retail outlet at the mall."

"What about the selling price? Is it reasonable?"

"I don't know. She gave me two signed contracts. I haven't looked at them."

"You haven't looked at them?"

"I'm just the middle man. I don't care about the price."

Henry was silent for a moment.

"Weren't you curious?"

"No."

Henry didn't sound pleased or relieved, but he said, "I guess we should thank you."

"You don't have to. I enjoy the game."

"I'll call Ernie and Billy. Could you bring the contracts to the garden center tomorrow morning?"

"Sure."

"Billy or Ernie can pick them up and take it from there."

"See you tomorrow."

A light, misty rain had begun to fall. Lucas walked slowly back to Fay's house. His gray eyes echoed the dull gray of the clouds.

Jeanette had said, "You escaped. How can I escape?"

How can anyone?

He wiped the raindrops from his cheeks, as if they were tears.

That evening, after a dinner of soup and a sandwich, Lucas drove to Fulton on Route Forty-Six. The rain had ended, but the air was still heavy with moisture. He left the highway at the eastern edge of town and followed a narrow country road north for several miles, past empty fields and shadowed woods.

It was dark when he pulled over onto the shoulder, not far from a small, shabby house planted near a few acres of farmland. A battered pick-up truck was parked near the barn.

He turned off the engine and sat in the warm, damp darkness, staring at the house, wondering what it would be like to live there and work there, day after day. Were these people happy? Did their children leave as soon as they could, the way he had left his home town?

The house stared back at him through two first-floor windows, the only windows that weren't dark.

Was someone sitting at one of those dark windows, looking out at the night? His mother used to do that, after his father died. She used to sit in her bedroom by the window, in the dark, for hours sometimes. The street they lived on was quiet, even during the day, like most small-town streets. There was nothing to see, no one to see. At night, it was deserted. But she sat there, night after night.

When Lucas was thirteen, he had a strange notion that his mother had lied to him, that his father's funeral was a lie, too. That she knew he wasn't really dead, that he had just run away for a while, for a long vacation from his family. That she was waiting for him to come back. And suddenly, in the middle of the night maybe, he would be there, a little older, but refreshed and ready to be a husband and a father again.

By the time he was eighteen, Lucas had left home, and he

never looked back or came back, until his mother's funeral. He never asked her why she sat there in the dark. And he was sure she wouldn't have told him.

He watched the farmhouse for almost an hour, the way his mother had watched the street outside their house.

He wondered, What was he waiting for?

On the way back to Pennington, Lucas stopped for a drink on Route Forty-Six, at a place called The Bar None.

It was a long, somber, dimly-lit room. A few empty tables were scattered along one wall, opposite a dark-wooden bar, at which three men and a woman were nursing their drinks. The men were sitting together, arguing seriously but casually, the way drinking buddies argue. The woman, a tall, sturdy, fortyish blonde in a black dress, was alone. The bartender was a scruffy young man in an even scruffier apron. There was a juke box against the back wall. It was playing a mournful Johnny Cash song.

Lucas sat two stools away from the woman and ordered a beer.

The first cold mouthfuls washed away some of the heat and dampness of the night.

He was tired of planning, tired of pretending, tired of remembering; so tired he could have put his head down on the bar and fallen asleep. And he knew that it would be a sleep without dreams—not peaceful, but cold and empty, like death.

Diana had once told him that the only thing she was afraid of was pain.

"Death doesn't scare me," she said. "But dying does. I saw my brother die. Slowly. He was just a kid, fifteen. He got hurt in a skiing accident, broke his back. It broke his spirit. He took a long time to die. Thank God he did, finally. I want it to be quick."

I guess I did her a favor.

He ordered another beer.

The woman looked at him, appraised him with a practiced eye and asked, "Just passing through?"

Her voice was harsh and raw, like an open wound.

"That's a good guess."

"Where are you headed?"

"One never knows."

She smiled wearily.

"A mystery man, huh? I've met a few of those before."

"Not every mystery is worth solving."

"Listen, I'm not in the mood for sex tonight. And my ex-husband is always on time with my alimony, so I can buy my own drinks. Can we just have a little conversation?"

Lucas moved over to sit next to her.

"I'm not much of a talker," he said.

"Why not?"

"The less people know about you, the harder it is for them to hurt you."

"Jesus, that's a hell of a way to look at things."

"It's true, isn't it?"

She frowned and examined him more carefully.

"Not everybody is out to get you."

"But how do you tell the good guys from the bad ones?"

She laughed. "I've been asking myself that question, all my life."

"I rest my case."

She extended her hand.

"My name is Karen."

He shook her hand.

"You can call me Max."

"Call me Max? Still being mysterious, huh?"

"Do you live in Fulton, Karen?"

"No. Exeter. I work at the college."

"You're a teacher?"

She laughed.

"Jesus, no! I barely got through high school. I work in the registrar's office. Word processing, filing."

"And you hang out at The Bar None on weekends?"

She shook her head.

"I don't usually go out on Sunday nights, but tonight I was restless. I got in my car and started to drive around. I stopped here. I don't know why."

"Same with me."

"You don't live around here, do you?"

"Why do you say that?"

"You look like you belong somewhere else."

"Where do you think that is?"

"I don't know. Someplace more exciting, I guess."

"You sound like you'd rather be somewhere else, too."

"Not me. I've had enough excitement in my life."

"That makes two of us."

The juke box played its last song.

"Do you have any quarters?" Karen asked. "This place is too quiet without music."

Lucas found three in his pocket.

"Thanks. You want to help me pick out the songs?"

"Play whatever you like. It doesn't matter to me."

By the time she came back to the bar, Billy Joel was singing "The Piano Man."

Lucas asked, "How long have you been divorced?"

"Seven—no, eight years."

"Does he still live in town?"

"Sure. He sees the kids a lot. And we run into each other all the time."

"Is that a problem?"

"No. He's a good man. We're still friends."

"So why'd you split up?"

"Bob wants to be looked up to. He wants to be admired. When I was young—I was sixteen when I married him—I thought he was hot shit. But you're only sixteen for a year. I grew up."

"That happens to the best of us."

"Not to Bob. He didn't want to change. And he sure as hell didn't want *me* to change. He got married again a couple of years ago, to a girl who's the spitting image of me when I was her age."

"How old are your kids?"

"My son is eighteen. He's a freshman at Exeter. He lives at home, and I don't have to pay tuition. You know, because I work there."

"That's a good deal. What about your daughter?"

"She's sixteen. I'm worried about her."

"Why?"

"Why does anyone worry about a sixteen-year-old girl? Men, of course."

"Boys will be boys."

"Yeah, but they're not the ones who get knocked up."

"You've warned her all about it, I'm sure."

"She doesn't listen."

"You might be smarter to stop talking."

"And watch her go down the drain? No way."

"Sometimes the more you do, the worse it gets."

"I'm not the quiet type."

"A guy I knew. Had an eighteen-year-old daughter. Wouldn't let her get married. Her boyfriend was a photographer. Wrote poetry. Barely made a living. Wanted to take her to California. Her father said, 'No.'"

"He was right."

"The photographer went to California. The girl spent the next ten years making her father miserable. Bumming around. And making damn sure he knew all about it."

"Is this guy you?"

"No. I was too busy for my daughter."

"That's too bad."

"She turned out fine. Proves my point."

"Sorry: no sale."

"She's better off now than she would have been if I had been there."

"Is she happier?"

"Happiness isn't everything."

"Jesus, you sure have a depressing way of looking at things."

"Just being honest."

"You're a hard case. Give yourself a break."

"Maybe I don't deserve it."

"Does anyone?"

Lucas finished his beer and motioned to the bartender.

"I'll take care of the lady's tab, too."

"Thanks."

"Good night."

"It can only go uphill from here," she said.

On the way back to Pennington, Lucas took a detour past Margot's house. He wanted to stop, but he didn't.

22

The Victory Dinner

On Monday morning, Lucas arrived at the garden center a few minutes after nine.

Leo was at the counter.

"So you pulled it off. Billy and Ernie got here an hour ago. They're in the office with Henry."

"Celebrating?"

"It's funny. They look more worried now than they did before. What the hell's the matter with them?"

"They still have to get Hamilton to agree. And Emily's offer is 'take it or leave it.'"

"But she didn't say, no."

"They're also worried about me."

Leo laughed.

"I can't say I blame them."

"They keep thinking, 'What's he getting out of this? Did he and Emily cook up a secret deal between them?'"

"Did you?"

"No."

"They can't believe you'd do something like this just for the hell of it."

"Can you?"

"Yeah, I can."

"See you later."

On his way to Henry's office, Lucas poured himself a cup of coffee.

Henry was sitting behind his desk, watching the door. Ernie was standing by the window, hands in his pockets. Billy was pacing up and down, rubbing his bald head vigorously, as if trying to coax a reluctant genie out of a magic lamp.

"Here he is," Henry said.

Billy stopped in his tracks.

Lucas dropped the Schuyler Enterprises envelope on Henry's desk.

Billy picked it up, opened it and took out one of the contracts. He read it quickly, page after page, nodding, frowning, mumbling "uh-huhs." Ernie came over to the desk and began looking through the other copy. Henry kept his eye on Lucas.

After a few minutes, Billy said, "It looks pretty good. I've already spoken to Jim Hamilton. He knows Emily wants a piece of the action. And I think her price will be acceptable."

Ernie wasn't as sure.

"That's a lot of money. I thought she'd come in a little lower."

He sounded breathless and disappointed, as if he had just lost a long-distance race.

"What do you think, Lucas?" Henry asked.

"It's out of my hands."

"But do you think Hamilton will agree?"

"I don't know. I've never met the man."

Henry took off his glasses and rubbed his eyes. He seemed

to be losing interest in the contract.

"I have an eleven o'clock appointment with Hamilton," Billy said. "Any words of wisdom?"

"Do you want me to go with you?" Ernie asked.

"No. I don't want to change the pattern. I'm the only one Jim knows. I think he'll be more comfortable if it's just me."

Henry put on his glasses, adjusted them, looked at Lucas.

"I'll see you at one o'clock, Henry," Lucas said. "Good luck, Billy."

On Wednesday morning, about ten o'clock, Fay left for Providence. A few minutes later, Joey knocked on the door of Lucas's apartment.

"Well, she's gone," Joey said, leaning against the door frame.

"I guess you're my landlord now."

"Yeah. But I'm still not sure why she left."

"Did you ask her?"

"Yeah. A change of scenery. A better job."

"That makes sense."

"But she didn't want that until you came here."

"I just reminded her that there's more to the world than Pennington."

"Maybe."

"You want a cup of coffee?"

"No. I've got to go to work."

Late that afternoon, Lucas was at the counter with Leo. It had been a slow day. Henry was in his office.

"Henry doesn't seem to care about the factory project any more," Leo said. "After all the talk about it."

"He may have something else on his mind."

"Do you know what it is?"

"Not really."

Leo studied Lucas for a moment before he said, "You're beginning to look like a man who's ready to hit the road again."

Lucas nodded.

"It'll be soon."

"Did Fay leave yet?"

"This morning."

"She was wasting her time in this town."

"What about you, Leo?"

"Honestly, I've been thinking about it."

"Back to your old life?"

"No. Just someplace else."

Henry appeared at the door to his office and motioned for Lucas to join him. He closed the door behind them.

"Jim Hamilton signed the contract," Henry said.

"Shouldn't you be smiling about that?"

"I suppose I should. Billy has invited you to dinner tomorrow night. Seven o'clock at his place. A celebration."

"I'll be there."

Billy Miles lived in a narrow, fifty-year-old Cape Cod house south of Route Forty-Six, at the western edge of the Glade. The dark cedar shingles were cracked and weathered. A massive, hump-backed oak tree dominated the narrow front yard and hovered over the roof like a disgruntled guardian angel.

Lucas rang the bell twice before Billy answered, smiling nervously.

"Come in, come in, Lucas."

Billy led the way into the living room, which was small to begin with, and so crowded with furniture, tables, shelves and knickknacks, that it seemed even smaller. Although there were several lamps in the room, most of their light was absorbed by the clutter. Nothing but the cold, gray half-light of a winter sunset remained.

There were too many paintings on the wall, unpleasant pictures of people and places that had never existed. A gloomy, faux tapestry covered one side of the room with a vaguely medieval battle scene. On a table beneath the tapestry, two bronze busts stared at each other across an ornate vase filled with artificial flowers.

The dinner guests who had arrived earlier—Henry on a chair in a dark corner, Ernie and Nadine on a stiff, brocade-covered love seat—were barely visible.

"Hello, Nadine. Ernie. Henry. Did you invite Don and Luther?"

"No. If we had a bigger dining room, we might have," Billy replied.

Lucas laughed.

"You're just giving Luther another excuse to get angry."

"So be it," Billy said. "Would you like a drink, Lucas?"

"A beer would do."

Billy returned with an Oktoberfest mug. Lucas raised it high. "Why so sad, folks? We made the sale."

Ernie said, hesitantly, "I don't know. It's taken so long—"

Billy interrupted, "And she still came out way ahead of us."

"You knew that from the start," Lucas said.

"They should have given us more," Ernie hissed. "Damn it, they should have."

"Emily had nothing to do with that."

"Don't you believe it," Ernie said, breathlessly.

"What did Hamilton give you?"

"What did Emily give *you*?" Ernie asked.

"Nothing."

"Nothing?"

Nadine put a calming hand on Ernie's arm. He looked down at her twisted, arthritic fingers as if they were a reminder of his own pain.

At that moment, a stocky, dark-haired woman entered the living room.

"Lucas, this is my wife, Helen," Billy said.

"Nice to meet you, Helen."

"They'd love to know how you did it," she said.

Her voice was detached and disinterested, as if she were talking about an event that had happened years ago to people she had never met.

"Just dumb luck, I guess."

"Luck has nothing to do with it," she said. "Emily is a clever bitch."

Helen's face would have been pretty if there were any warmth in it. But her eyes were lifeless, and she moved sluggishly.

"What's the difference? She agreed to sell the factory."

"Tell us how you did it."

Lucas was too tired to pretend.

"She likes to win. I showed her how to make a deal and still come out a winner."

"Damn!" Ernie said. "Damn!"

"We won, too," Billy whispered, as if he were afraid to be heard.

"That's right," Lucas said.

Helen watched Lucas for a moment. "But why did she even listen to you?"

"You'd have to ask her."

"They should have given us more," Ernie repeated.

"What did you get?" Lucas asked.

Ernie frowned.

"A hundred grand," Henry replied.

"A piece?"

"No, no, no," Ernie sighed.

"That's not bad."

"It's not enough," Ernie said. "Do you know how much Emily sold that damn factory for?"

"I have no idea."

Helen raised her hand.

"Dinner is ready."

Billy hadn't exaggerated: there was just enough room for six at the dinner table. Billy sat at the head, Helen at the side nearest the door to the kitchen, with Ernie beside her. Nadine and Lucas sat on the other side, and Henry sat at the foot, across from Billy.

As the wooden salad bowl was being passed around, Lucas said to Helen, "Your son and I work together every day."

"He doesn't actually do any work, does he?"

"As little as possible."

"That's the way young people are these days," Billy said, trying to smile.

"That's the way he's always been. That's the way he'll always be," Helen added.

"Well, Henry doesn't seem to mind," Lucas said.

Helen didn't respond.

"Henry's pretty tough on everyone else. But he treats Billy, Jr., differently."

"Does he?"

"Better."

"We appreciate that," Billy said.

Helen looked at Billy, at Lucas, but not at Henry—not then, and only once that evening. For several moments, no one spoke.

Henry broke the silence.

"Joey says Fay left town."

Lucas nodded.

"She went to Providence. Got a job there as a librarian. At an insurance company."

"It didn't take you long to scare her off," Henry said.

"I didn't think I was that scary."

"You're not," Nadine said. "Not at all."

Lucas smiled at her.

"Come on. How about a victory toast?" Lucas asked.

"Victory?" Ernie said. "By the time we pay our taxes, we won't clear enough to make a difference."

"Money doesn't change who you are, Ernie," Lucas said.

"But it changes what you can do."

Lucas raised his glass and toasted, "To victory."

23

Confessor

Henry wasn't at work when Lucas showed up on Friday afternoon.

"How was the celebration last night?" Leo asked.

"It was more like a funeral."

"And no one thanked you, right?"

"Right."

"Amazing!"

"Was Henry here this morning?"

"He called. He's taking the day off."

Lucas smiled.

"Success is a cruel master," Leo said.

"Ain't it, though?"

Late that night, Lucas walked over to Henry's house and rang the doorbell.

Henry almost smiled, when he saw him.

"Come in."

Henry was wearing chino workpants and a dark blue, knit shirt.

"You look like you've been expecting me."

"I have."

There was no aggression in Henry's voice or manner.

Lucas followed him into the living room.

They sat facing each other.

"I understand my dream now," Lucas said.

Henry remained silent.

"I understand why you're in my dream."

"And you're going to tell me about it."

Henry was speaking softly, almost passively. He leaned back in his chair and folded his arms loosely across his chest.

"Go ahead."

"The minister in my dream is you."

"Yes, that's what you said."

"He preaches to an empty church."

"Yes."

"That's because he's lost his faith."

"Yes."

"He tells me that there is a Devil, but no God. Sin, but no salvation."

"No salvation," Henry said, softly.

"He welcomes me to Hell."

"I remember that."

"Last night, when I went home, I couldn't fall asleep until late, very late. And I had the dream again. But this time, it was different."

Lucas hesitated, trying to gauge Henry's mood.

"In the dream, I called out your name from the back of the church. And you came running down the aisle. You got down on

238

your knees in front of me. And you shouted, 'Forgive me!' As if *I* was the minister."

Lucas paused.

"And I asked, 'How have you sinned?' But you didn't answer me."

Henry seemed calm, almost apathetic.

"Then you reached out toward me."

Lucas leaned forward, his hand toward Henry.

"And you shouted, again, 'Forgive me!'"

Henry looked at Lucas's hand and waited.

"I said, 'Confess your sins.' And then I woke up."

Lucas took a deep breath.

"Finally, I understand what the dream means."

Lucas listened to the silence for a moment.

"I understand, Henry."

"I've never lost my faith."

"Why did you leave the seminary?"

Henry stood up and turned away.

"I didn't feel the calling any more."

Lucas stood up.

"That's not why you left."

Henry turned to face Lucas. His eyes began to catch fire.

"You don't know anything about me."

"But I know how you've sinned."

"You don't know!"

Lucas put his hand on Henry's shoulder.

"Tell me."

Henry pulled away from him.

"Why should I tell you anything?"

"Isn't confession good for the soul?"

"Leave me alone."

"You'll feel better if you tell me . . ."

"I have nothing to confess."

Lucas moved closer and spoke softly. "Does anyone else know? Anyone besides Helen, I mean."

Henry's eyes flashed darkly. He lunged at Lucas, awkwardly swinging his right fist. Lucas blocked the punch with his left arm, and hit Henry in the stomach.

Henry fell to his knees, gasping for breath.

"The minister got down on his knees in front of me."

Henry looked up at him.

"What do you want?"

"Helen won't come to your Bible classes. And she never goes to church. She's lost her faith, hasn't she?"

Henry moaned.

"Why did she lose her faith?"

"I don't know."

"Yes, you do."

Henry shook his head.

"Why does she hate you?"

"She doesn't."

"Tell me about Billy, Jr."

Henry bowed lower, his face almost touching the floor.

"Billy, Jr., isn't anything like his father, is he?" Lucas said.

Henry sat back on his haunches and looked up at Lucas.

"Why do you think he's so different from his father, Henry?"

"I don't know."

"Why do you let Billy, Jr., get away with everything?"

Henry said nothing.

Lucas leaned down and put one hand on each of Henry's shoulders, and held him tightly.

"I know why Billy, Jr., isn't like his father."

Henry tried to turn away.

"Tell me, Henry. Tell me."

Henry began to sob.

"Tell me. I swear no one else will ever know."

Lucas crouched down and let go of Henry's shoulders.

Henry stopped crying. His tears had quenched the fire in his eyes.

"Helen and I had talked about marriage. But when I got the letter from the seminary, when they accepted me, I knew there was no room in my life for anything else. I couldn't get married. Maybe later, I told her. But I didn't ask her to wait for me. Maybe I should have."

He clasped his hands.

"She didn't wait. She married Billy. I didn't come back to Pennington until I had finished my second year. My mother was still alive then, but she didn't have much use for religion, or for me. So why should I go home?"

Henry held his clasped hands against his chest.

"It was in the summer. I didn't try to see Helen."

Remembering, he smiled.

"But I met her by accident at the diner one morning. We had breakfast together."

His smile faded.

"She wasn't happy. I could see that. She blamed me. She said so. She said I shouldn't have left her. She said that she and Billy were trying to start a family, but they couldn't."

He raised his clasped hands, closed his eyes, and began to sway from side to side.

"I was weak."

"Did you love her?"

"Not any more. But we had never . . . I wanted her."

"So you gave her a child."

"I gave her a child. A child she hates because he's my child."

Henry opened his eyes.

"Because I left her and she married someone she didn't love."

"So you lost your faith. And she lost hers."

Lucas stood up and looked down at Henry.

"I've never lost my faith," Henry said. "But I lost my right to preach the faith."

Henry unclasped his hands. He breathed in deeply and suddenly seemed at peace.

"I think Billy is the only one who loves that boy," he said. "The only one who forgives him."

"And who will forgive you?"

24

The Greenhouse

On Saturday morning, at a few minutes before seven o'clock, Lucas took a long walk around Pennington.

He had found what he wanted to find. He knew he would be leaving soon. He tried to step back and look at the town again from a distance, the way he had looked at it on the first day. But he couldn't.

His final stop was the Cascades. He walked slowly through the dew-wet grass, ran for a half mile or so, and then walked again, into the woods, searching for Jeanette's wind chimes, but he couldn't find them.

She hadn't called. He wanted to see her again, hear her voice again, before he left. But he probably wouldn't.

At nine-thirty, back at the apartment, Lucas was finishing his second cup of breakfast coffee when there was a knock at the door. He couldn't believe Joey was up this early on a weekend.

"Good morning, Mr. Murdoch," Jeanette said.

Her expression was an odd mixture of tension and serenity.

"May I come in for a moment?"

"Sure. Would you like a cup of coffee, or . . .?"

She shook her head.

"I can't stay. There's a car waiting for me."

She was wearing a pale blue summer dress that softened the slim lines of her body. Her eyes seemed softer, too.

"Where are you going?"

"Grandmother is sending me away to school."

"Far away?"

"Far enough. The school is called Wyndham Oaks. It's in a suburb of Philadelphia."

"How did you get her to do that?"

"I thought about what you told me. And I found a way to hurt her," she said, laughing. "I massacred all of her darling little flowers. When I got through with the greenhouse, it looked as if it had been hit by Hurricane Jeanette."

Lucas smiled.

"She can replace all of that," he said.

"Of course she can. It isn't the dead flowers that made her angry. It's the fact that I betrayed her."

"So she's sending you away."

"Grandmother says it's a very strict school. Girls only, of course. She says they'll teach me how to be a lady."

"It sounds charming."

"Grandmother was a student there. She donates a lot of money to the school. She's on the board of trustees."

"I guess that means they'll give you the star treatment."

"No doubt about it. Solitary confinement, bread and water, chains and whips."

"That kind of thing builds character."

Jeanette frowned.

"Grandmother said that Wyndham Oaks was the right school for her, and it will be for me, too, because we're so much alike. We're not alike, are we?"

"What she means is that you're just as strong as she is. She's sure of that now. That's the only way you two are alike."

"Maybe I'll turn out just the way she did."

"No, you won't."

"I hope not."

"She never climbed up in a tree to dream about things, or listen to wind chimes."

Jeanette studied Lucas for a moment.

"That's a kind thing to say."

She looked around the apartment.

"This is a pretty grim little place. It would be a perfect setting for a Camus novel."

"You're the Camus expert."

She nodded.

"Have you been banished for life?"

"I guess that depends on me. You didn't pick out this furniture, did you?"

Lucas laughed.

"Don't worry about it. I'm not going to be here much longer."

"Where are you going?"

"I'm not sure."

"You never told me why you came to Pennington. Why you decided not to be Max Murdock any more. Will you tell me someday?"

"We may not know each other someday."

"Yes, we will," she said, softly.

"Jeanette . . ."

"Wyndham Oaks is going to be a terrible place for me."

"It'll be a breeze. You're smarter and you know more than anyone there, including the teachers. You'll leave them in the dust."

She shook her head.

"I'm not used to being with other people, particularly young people. That's the whole point of a place like that. It's not about learning. It's about behavior. There won't be any trees to climb. No wind chimes. No place to hide. That scares me."

"You'll be fine."

"I will be, if I have someone to think about. Someone who cares about me."

"Your grandmother . . ."

"Someone to call when I'm feeling discouraged, or lonely. Not Grandmother."

There was no veil over her eyes, no half-smile. Lucas tried to look away, but couldn't.

"I need to think of you as my friend, even if you're far away."

"I *am* your friend."

Her eyes filled with tears.

"I need someone to love," she said.

"I'm not someone to love. Believe me."

"But you're all I've got."

"Call me, whenever you need to."

25

The Demon

Lucas stood by the open door for a minute or two after Jeanette left. Then he sat down at the table and drained the cold coffee in the mug, slowly, pensively.

He went into the bedroom, took his two suitcases out of the closet, put one on the bed and opened it, but left it there and returned to the living room. He paced up and down, feeling restless and uneasy. Why had he made that offer to Jeanette?

His memories of Pennington, like the memories of his whole life, were chaotic and confused, a jigsaw puzzle he couldn't solve.

He went out onto the patio and sat at the table.

It was a warm, sweet-smelling morning. Spring was just beginning to become summer.

He tried to feel the warmth, but couldn't.

Beth had said, "I don't need you any more, Daddy. And I never will."

Emily, alone in the emptiness of the Grange, would never forgive Lucas for what Jeanette had done to her.

There were so many sins, so many nevers.

No matter where he went, there would always be too many sins, too many nevers.

By five-thirty that afternoon, he had packed. He ate a ham sandwich and three chocolate chip cookies, drinking the last of the milk straight from the container. He emptied the refrigerator and the pantry, and tossed everything into one of the garbage cans in back of the house. He put the suitcases in the trunk of his car, left the key to the apartment on the dining room table, and drove south onto Route Forty-Six, then east toward Fulton.

He didn't have a final destination in mind. He thought he might drive up to the coast of Maine, walk on the beach, watch the ocean, and decompress for a while. Or he might find a place by a lake in New Hampshire. Not Vermont, of course. Never Vermont.

He passed the deserted factory, still a haunted wasteland, soon to become the Schuyler Shopping Center; another victory for Emily, another defeat for Billy and Ernie.

In Fulton, he passed Memory Lane. He tried not to remember the night he met Margot there, but he could see her face, hear her voice, feel the slender softness of her body.

When he saw the sign for The Bar None, Lucas decided to stop for a drink.

The place looked even shabbier in daylight. A handful of customers sat at the bar and at a couple of tables. The juke box was silent. The bartender on duty was a young woman dressed in tight black slacks and a long-sleeved white shirt, a little too small for her. Lucas thought he had seen her before, but he couldn't remember where.

He ordered a beer.

When she brought it to him, she smiled and he remembered.

He said, "You were at the fights in St. Albans last Friday."

She nodded.

"Selena, I think."

She smiled again.

"Selena, yes."

"I guess you're a local celebrity."

"It's a couple of extra bucks for showing my legs to a bunch of guys who've known me since I was a kid." She shrugged. "If it makes them happy . . ."

"I guess it does."

"I was spending a lot of time at boxing matches anyway. My husband was a fighter. So Jeff Barclay—he's the beer distributor around here, and he bankrolls the St. Albans promoter—he says he'll give me a hundred bucks a night to be the round-card girl. Every little bit helps."

"Was your husband on the card last week?"

"He doesn't fight any more."

One of the customers at the far end of the bar called her name.

"I'll be back in a minute," she said.

When she returned, Lucas asked, "Did your husband stay in the business?"

"No. He's a mechanic at the Texaco station a couple of miles down the road. We're saving up for our own gas station. We'll have enough money in a couple of years."

"Was he any good? As a fighter, I mean."

"He was damn good. Artie Madison is his name. He was a middleweight. Had a twenty-two and two record. Eighteen knockouts. He had a beautiful left hook, like De La Hoya. In fact, he was on the undercard at Madison Square Garden when De La Hoya beat—who was it?—Jesse James Leija."

"Did Artie win that night, too?"

She paused.

"Yeah, but . . ."

"But what?"

"I've known Artie since we were kids. We never dated anyone else. He's a good man, you know?"

Lucas nodded.

"But the fighter part of him . . ."

She waved both of her hands as if to wipe away a false image, and added, "I mean, he would never touch me, or the kids, or anything. But even back in school, when he was pushed, he pushed back harder, a lot harder. And in the ring, it's like he doesn't feel any pain. He just keeps going after the other guy until he nails him. I used to tell him that he had—I called it a demon—and it was hiding inside him. And when he was in a fight, the demon took over."

"It sounds like the demon had a great record. Why did Artie quit?"

"That night at the Garden, the night of the De La Hoya fight, Artie almost killed a guy. Kept hitting him when he was down. The guy's never been the same. Can hardly talk. They suspended Artie for six months, but it didn't matter to him. He wouldn't go back in the ring again."

"These things happen."

"We talked all night after that fight. He told me he was afraid of that thing inside him. That he needed me to help him keep it locked up. He needs me, and I need him, too."

She suddenly looked embarrassed.

"I talk too much. I mean, bartenders are supposed to *listen*, right?" She smiled. "Do you want to tell me your troubles?"

"I don't have any troubles."

"Lucky you. Do you want another beer?"

He nodded.

She brought the beer quickly and walked to the opposite

end of the bar without saying another word.

Lucas thought, Artie needs her to help keep the demon locked up.

Lucas knew the demon, too.

He finished the beer and left a twenty dollar bill on the bar.

26

The Storm

Lucas spent the next two weeks at a motel on the Maine coast, south of Cape Elizabeth—ten whitewashed cabins at the edge of a narrow, rocky beach. The motel shared a quiet inlet with a general store, and with Mike's, a locally popular seafood restaurant. The water in the inlet was surprisingly calm, but much too cold for swimming.

There was a small refrigerator, an electric coffee-maker, a toaster and a hot plate in the cabin, so Lucas could make breakfast for himself. He usually had a mid-day lunch/dinner at the restaurant.

Every morning, he would get up early, drink some juice and coffee, and then run for as long as he could on the hard-packed, water-soaked strip of beach closest to the ocean. He had to fight a cold northeast wind that tried to slow him down, discourage him, stop him in his tracks. He made sure to run further every morning.

When he reached that day's limit, he would walk back to the motel, shower, go to the general store, buy the *Portland Press Herald*, and read the newspaper while he ate breakfast.

He had picked up an armful of books in Kennebunkport—spy stories, detective stories, with twists and turns that would keep his mind busy, that would keep him from thinking about himself.

The other guests at the motel were sport fishermen, whose power-boats were tied up at the dock. They left early in the morning and stayed out until sundown.

At dusk one day, Lucas went out onto the beach for an evening walk. A middle-aged, gray-haired man had set up an easel a few yards from the ocean and was sitting on a wooden stool, palette in hand, brushing colors onto a rectangular canvas. Lucas looked over his shoulder.

Although the painting was still in its early stages, the artist had already captured the cold half-light that hovered over the water, and the loneliness of the rocky beach.

"That's very good," Lucas said.

"Thanks." He laughed. "I wasn't catching much anyway."

"You came here to fish?"

"I just use that as an excuse to take some time off. To get away from the city for a while."

"Boston? New York?"

"New York. I can depressurize here."

He turned to look at Lucas.

"I've seen you running in the morning. I wish I was in such good shape."

"It doesn't take talent: just persistence."

"Aye, there's the rub."

Lucas pointed at the canvas.

"That takes talent."

"And persistence, too. I'm not really a great artist, but I make a pretty good living at it."

"Selling paintings?"

"I design ads, promotional pieces, brochures, that kind of thing. And now and then, I'll work on a painting like this, just for myself."

He rested the brush on the easel and extended his right hand.

"I'm Norm Schuster."

"Lucas Murdoch."

"You're not a fisherman, either."

"No. I'm just taking some time out."

"From what? If you don't mind me asking."

"I'm a consultant. Semi-retired. But I still like to keep my hand in."

Schuster nodded, looked at his canvas, then at the sky and the ocean.

"This is the most difficult time of day to capture. The dawn is a little easier, a little more tangible." He turned back to face Lucas again. "Not that actual sundowns are that hard. But this time of day, just before sundown, before the colors begin to percolate—that's very elusive."

Lucas tried to look at the scene through Norm Schuster's eyes.

"I was on a plane once, coming into New York City at dusk," Schuster recalled. "The light on the water and the bridges, and on the glass and steel and concrete, was amazing. It took my breath away. I was with a photographer friend of mine. And he said that he had caught the physical look of that moment a couple of times, but the feeling was always missing. He thought that our response to that kind of light wasn't just psychological. He thought it was atavistic."

"Atavistic?"

"Like a reflection of our racial memory."

"Racial memory?"

"My friend thought that when we were still living in caves,

we were afraid when we saw the sun set. Because we weren't sure that it would ever come up again. It did, every day, but we didn't know why. So how did we know that it would come back tomorrow? Now, when we see the sun dying, even though we know why, we still feel some of that old caveman fear."

"Maybe it has nothing to do with the sun. Maybe it's just dying that scares us."

"You're probably right about that."

"I'd better be going. You'll be running out of sunset soon."

"Right. And I'm leaving early tomorrow morning, so this is my last chance. It was nice meeting you, Lucas."

"Same here, Norm." Lucas smiled. "And now I know what atavistic means."

The next morning, while Lucas was running in bright sunshine, a dark shadow began to gather on the northeastern horizon. The wind in his face was razor-sharp and chilly.

By the time he got back to the motel, the shadow had become a fast-approaching storm cloud. The fishermen were returning to the dock, tying up their boats and running for cover.

Lucas stood on the beach and watched the cloud move toward him. It was a huge, black bug with lightning-bolt legs. Its breath was an icy wind, kicking up the waves. And now he could see the rain pouring out of it, pelting the ocean.

As the storm reached the beach, cold, angry shards of hail were hitting the sand and ricocheting off the rocks.

Lucas ran to his cabin, opened the door and looked back at the storm. The wind was so strong he had to shut his eyes. He pulled hard to shut the door.

He walked over to the window. The day had turned into

a starless, moonless night. A moment later there was the rattle of hailstone bullets on the roof, a rattle that became a roar as the cloud passed overhead.

Lucas thought of the cavemen, of their fear that the sun might never rise again. When it stormed like this, it must have seemed to them like the death of the world. They would have heard the angry voices of their gods in thunder and lightning, cursing them for their sins. And they would have prayed to the sun to forgive them.

Lucas understood the caveman's fear. And he wanted to feel it now, to substitute it for all of his other fears.

27

Wyndham Oaks

Late that afternoon, his cell phone rang.

"How are you doing, Lucas?" Jeanette asked, softly.

"I'm fine. How is school?"

"I got here just as the spring term was ending. It's been rather awkward, to say the least."

"No classes for you?"

"That's right. But the summer session begins in a week or so, and I'm signed up for that."

"What's it like?"

"Beautiful grounds. Beautiful classrooms. Beautiful dorms."

"It sounds like paradise."

"And there's an army of self-satisfied young women, strutting around like fashion models, speaking oh-so-beautifully and saying absolutely nothing."

"Not quite paradise."

"It's a little worse than I thought it would be."

"You'll make friends, Jeanette."

"I already have a room mate."

"Aha!"

"Her name is Annabelle Marquand."

"Sounds charming."

"She's already gone home for the summer."

"So, what's she like?"

"I don't know where to begin."

"Give it a try."

"She's a pale, fragile little person. Her eyes are too close together and her lips are too thin."

"She really does sound charming."

"Too much inbreeding, I think."

Lucas laughed.

"She moves in a strange way, in fits and starts. It's almost like watching a badly-edited movie."

"Is there more?"

"There's more. She speaks the way she moves. She'll start a sentence very quickly, then slow down for no apparent reason, and then pick up speed again."

"Anything else?"

"From what I can gather, her family has a perfect fortune."

"As does yours."

"Not really. Grandmother is a pauper compared to Annabelle's people."

"I'm impressed."

"So is everyone else here. She's very popular."

"Of course."

"Do you ever think of me?"

"Yes, I do."

"I think of you all the time. I miss you."

She waited, but he didn't respond.

"What's going on in Pennington? Has Grandmother sent out a posse to hang you from the nearest tree?"

"I'm not in Pennington any more."

"When did you leave?"

"About the same time you did."

"I understand: without me, Pennington just isn't the same."

"No doubt about that."

"I'm flattered. Where are you now? The Gobi Desert? The Canary Islands?"

"I'm in a little town on the coast of Maine."

"Do you plan to settle down there?"

"I'm not sure what my next stop will be."

"What are you up to, Lucas?"

"I promise I'll tell you someday."

"It doesn't make any difference to me, I love you anyway."

"I wish you didn't."

"Do *you* love anybody?"

"Let's talk about that some other time."

"All the rest of us poor mortals need love."

"I'm just a poor mortal, too."

"Grandmother isn't."

"You may be right about that."

"She called me a few days ago."

"Was she still angry?"

"Actually, even when she sent me into exile, she wasn't angry. She said she was (and I quote) 'disappointed,' and I think that's true."

"Why did she call you?"

"To assure me that Wyndham Oaks would solve all my problems. She virtually guaranteed that I would emerge a new, and much better, person."

"How did you handle that?"

"I was polite . . ."

"As you always are."

"And just as cold as she was. And I kept remembering how good I felt when I killed all of her dear little flowers."

He waited two or three beats before he said, "I miss you, too, Jeanette."

28

The Rose Garden

That night, Lucas ate a late dinner at Mike's. By that time, only a few tables were still occupied.

The morning's storm was a distant memory as he sat by the window and looked out at a clear, star-splashed sky.

Are the gods smiling again?

After he had finished a bowl of lobster bisque, Lucas dug into his pocket for his phone and dialed.

"Margot. It's Luke."

"I won't ask you where you've been. That's always a secret, isn't it?"

"I thought it would be better for you . . ."

"Better for me to fall in love with you and lose you?"

"I told you once that I hadn't planned on meeting you."

"I didn't plan to meet you, either."

"I want to be with you."

"For how long?"

"I don't know."

"That's the wrong answer, Luke."

"I didn't mean that the way it sounded. I want to tell you about myself. After that, maybe you won't want me."

He thought he heard her sigh.

"I've been alone too long," she said. "Then I met you. I didn't . . ."

"Can I come to see you?"

"I don't know."

"You don't have to decide now. I'm up in Maine, at a motel on the coast."

"Maine?"

"I can call you tomorrow, or . . ."

"When can you be here?"

"Tomorrow afternoon."

It was a little after three o'clock the next day when he pulled up in front of Margot's house.

On the lawn, a robin redbreast was digging for worms. A soft breeze brushed across his face as he rang the bell.

"Come in, Luke," Margot said in an even tone.

She was dressed in jeans, a pale green tee shirt and sandals. She looked so young to him. Or was it that he suddenly felt so old?

He followed her into the living room. She motioned to the couch and sat on a chair across from him, studying his face carefully for a moment, as if she were reconstructing a half-forgotten image.

"Something to drink?"

"No, thanks."

"You look like you've been out in the sun."

"Yes. I was at the beach for a couple of weeks."

"Why Maine?"

"I've been there before. It's a quiet place."

She nodded.

"When you came here that weekend. I never . . ."

So many nevers.

"Then, suddenly, a quick call and you're gone."

"It won't be that way again."

That night, sleeping beside Margot, Lucas dreamed of a different rose. The bushes, bursting with bright red blossoms, were neatly planted on both sides of a broad, smooth path. It was a warm, summer morning. The sun was still low on the horizon. A woman was walking toward him. The sun was behind her, shining so brightly that he couldn't see her face, even when she came close and embraced him. She pressed her face against his chest. He held her in his arms and kissed her hair.